One of the Crowd

By Rosamond du Jardin

One of the Crowd

By
ROSAMOND DU JARDIN

J. B. Lippincott Company
PHILADELPHIA · NEW YORK

jD 884c

j.D 884.

To my nieces
Gwen and Sheila
with the warmest affection

Contents

One of the Crowd

The Blow Falls

Midge Heydon sat hunched on the edge of Judy Allen's bed, watching her friend lackadaisically fold sweaters and blouses and underwear into a big suitcase. Late afternoon sunlight slanted through the windows but it did nothing to dispel the gloom that engulfed the two girls. Tall, blond Midge, whose face was usually quite cheerful, looked as though she were about to lose her best friend—which, indeed, she was. Shorter, dark-haired Judy paused frequently in her task to emit a sad, deep sigh.

Almost twenty-four hours had elapsed since Midge had heard the shattering and utterly unexpected news that the Allens were going to move away. And though she ached dully with the awareness of Judy's imminent departure, a part of her mind still stubbornly refused to accept it as true. If she had said, "Judy, you can't be going!" once, she must have said it half a dozen times. So there was no point in repeating the inane

11

words, even though she felt them rising irresistibly to her lips again.

Judy forestalled her by exclaiming, "The ghastly thing is the way my parents are so happy about it! Even if this advancement is a big deal for Dad and all, you'd think they'd have some consideration for me, instead of simply rushing me off by plane tomorrow as if—as if I were a chattel or something!"

So thoroughly had they hashed the whole situation over that Midge knew its every ramification almost as well as Judy did. Mrs. Allen had been born and raised in Cincinnati, the city to which they were moving. She had so many relatives and friends there, she wasn't in the least averse to leaving Edgewood, where her ties, though warm, had been of much shorter duration. The main problem had been Judy. Her parents, unwilling for her to start her sophomore year at Edgewood High and then have to make a change in a few weeks, had hit on the sensible solution of sending her off at once to stay with an aunt in Cincinnati. After all, school would start in a few days. And it made infinitely more sense for Judy to enroll in the city where she'd be living. Mr. and Mrs. Allen could attend to such details as selling their house and having their furniture moved and would join Judy as soon as possible. A long-distance phone call to the aunt in question had settled everything. By leaving Sunday, Judy would be all ready to start classes in Cincinnati on Monday morning.

"They're simply dragging you up by the roots," Midge commiserated. Fairness prodded her into adding, "Of course, under the circumstances, I guess there wasn't much else they could do."

"It's what my father gets for being an organization man," Judy said darkly. "Why couldn't he work for some nice local company instead of a big nationwide monster with branches in dozens of cities? I suppose as soon as I get all set in Cincinnati, they'll switch him somewhere else."

"Maybe not," Midge said. But it was hard to be comforting when she herself felt so terrible about Judy's leaving. They had been such close friends for so long, she couldn't even imagine what it would be like without Judy around to talk to. Sharing experiences was almost as much fun as having them in the first place. But if you had no close confidante, no one you could trust absolutely——the thought of it was scarcely to be borne. Midge said miserably, "I honestly don't know how I'm going to get along without you."

She meant it, too. Who but Judy knew her so well, understood her so completely, had stood by her during most of the major crises in her life? Judy, having been at Green Lake with her last summer, knew all about Tom Brooks and how Midge felt about him. Even though Tom lived a couple of hundred miles away in Indianapolis, Midge had by no means forgotten him. Not that she intended to go around comparing every boy she met with Tom. That wouldn't be fair; there were so few to equal him. His funny, sardonic grin and direct gray glance, his tall, lean figure topped by dark, close-cut hair, his dry wit and questing interest in practically everything—Midge felt all soft and warm inside just remembering. Then she remembered something else. The first few times she had encountered Tom, she hadn't been in the least impressed with him. She had thought him sarcastic and rude and not too good-looking. It only went to show you, she reflected with a faint smile, how foolish it was to make snap judgments.

"What," Judy demanded, "are you grinning about at a time like this?"

"I was thinking of Tom," Midge admitted, "and how my first impression of him was so awful."

"That was just because you were developing such an overwhelming crush on Lex at the time."

A little pain stabbed at Midge. Lex Gresham meant nothing to her now, nor had he for quite a while. Still, it would always hurt some, she supposed, to remember how hard she had fallen for his striking looks and winning personality and how bitterly disillusioning it had been to learn he was just a conceited phony.

"Don't remind me what a dope I was," Midge said. "I was just thinking what a mistake it is to think you like, or dislike, a person before you actually have a chance to know him."

"Well, sure," Judy agreed. "Who's arguing? I'd love to get to know any number of boys really well. As well, for instance, as you know Bob Pierson."

"Oh, no, not that well!" Midge shook her head. "When you can remember how a boy looked in third grade, you just can't get excited over him, even when he's old enough to wear a tuxedo and bring you a corsage."

14

"Even so," Judy said, "he's better than nothing."

Midge knew she was thinking about that ridiculous offer of Bob's to take her to any high school affair for which she didn't have a more exciting date. He had made it out of gratitude because she had helped him acquire an ancient car which had been moldering for years in Miss Tess Wentworth's carriage house. And Midge hadn't the remotest intention of taking him up on it. But Judy couldn't seem to get that through her head.

"I've told you and told you——" Midge began irately.

"I know," Judy broke in. "Still, you have to admit it's just like having insurance. If you get invited to things by someone else, fine. If you don't, there's always Bob to fall back on. The only trouble would be," she frowned, "if you go out with him too often, the idea might get around that you're going steady."

"That's all I need!" Midge snorted derisively.

"But you know how it is at school," Judy warned. "If you date the same boy two or three times, everybody assumes——"

"I *know* how it is," Midge assured her. "And I won't date Bob often enough to take the slightest chance."

Suddenly dull gloom settled over Judy's face. She spoke almost accusingly. "It isn't going to be nearly as bad for you as it will for me! You'll be in the same school, among people you know. But I'll be lost in a crowd of utter strangers!"

Midge nodded sympathetically. "Hasn't this aunt of yours any children? Maybe they can help you make friends."

15

"Hah!" Judy emitted a hollow, unmirthful laugh. "Big help they'll be. They're all in grade school. I can just see us getting terribly chummy." She tried to crush a pleated skirt into the already-beginning-to-overflow suitcase, then raised tragic eyes to Midge's face. "I can't even take all my clothes along! Mother says this one suitcase will have to do me until they can send the rest of my stuff by express. I'll probably find I've forgotten something vital and can't even get decently dressed for school Monday!"

The thought occurred to Midge that Judy was rather enjoying her role of abused heroine. She tried to brush the suspicion aside, but couldn't quite seem to. After all, she knew that if she were in Judy's shoes there would be a certain excited expectancy buried somewhere underneath her normal unwillingness to leave familiar surroundings. Deep down within her, Midge reflected, would glow a faint but persistent hope that perhaps in a new school there would be a boy more wonderful than any boy she'd known before, one who would be absolutely dazzled by the charms of a new girl.

"You'll look just fine," she assured Judy. "Don't worry."

"Well, I won't feel fine," Judy said dismally. "Just think, I won't know a soul in the whole school. It was bad enough last year. Why, just talking with a boy in the corridor used to put me into a purple panic. I was scared I'd say the wrong things and bore him and that made me so confused I couldn't think of anything to say at all."

"I felt the same way," Midge admitted. "But we've both grown a little more self-confident. We have a better idea of how to make boys like us and ask us for dates. Knowing Roger and Tom did that for us."

Midge saw at once that it had been a mistake to mention Roger, the boy Judy had liked so well at Green Lake. Her friend's face seemed to crumple as she demanded, "If we had to move to Ohio, why couldn't it have been to Cleveland? Then I'd have had Roger. But Cincinnati's not much closer to Cleveland than Edgewood is."

"Maybe you'll meet someone else as nice, or even nicer, than Roger," Midge tried to comfort her.

But Judy was determined not to look on the bright side. "I probably won't have a single date my whole sophomore year. If I were staying here, we could help each other and compare notes and—sort of learn about boys together. But I'll be all alone."

"I'll be all alone too," Midge reminded her regretfully.

"No, you won't," Judy shook her head. "You know lots of other girls. You won't be just starting from scratch."

"Yes, but practically everyone has a real close friend by the time she's in high school," Midge said. "It won't be easy for me, either. I know I can't find anyone like you."

"Oh, Midge," Judy gulped. "What are we going to do?"

"I guess," Midge sighed, "we'll just have to—discuss things by letter and—get along the best we can. . . ."

17

CHAPTER 2

Friends Must Part

Midge and Judy said their last good-bys that evening. Judy's parents were driving her to Chicago to catch her plane early the next morning. Midge moped around most of that Sunday, despite her mother's and father's efforts to cheer her.

"After all," Dad said, "it isn't as if she'd taken off for the moon. You can certainly arrange to see each other during the Christmas holidays or, at the latest, next summer."

"But that's so far away," Midge said. "Why, only Friday night, when Judy slept here, we were talking about all the fun we were going to have this year at school."

"But you can still have fun——" Dad began.

Mom interrupted gently, "Now, Henry, you just don't understand. It's a shattering experience to lose a close girl friend, especially so suddenly. Girls need someone to talk things over with more than boys do,

18

a friend they can trust with their secrets. I can remember feeling like that."

"Yes, but can't she make friends with another girl? There are dozens of teen-age girls around."

"Of course," Mom agreed, "but it takes time."

"Besides," Midge added, "most friendships are pretty well set by the time you reach my age. They've sort of grown and developed over the years, just as Judy's and mine did. I can't just go up to someone, tap her on the shoulder and say, 'Let's be friends.' It's not that simple."

Dad sighed and went back to his perusal of the Sunday paper. His sigh said plainly that he did not understand women and never expected to, even though he'd had four daughters and had lived surrounded by females for years. Midge's eyes and Mom's met knowingly. The realization of her mother's sympathy made Midge feel a little better, but not much.

"Why don't you call up someone?" Dad suggested around the edge of the paper. "Ask someone over or—something?"

Midge didn't really want to brood. Still, she honestly couldn't think of a single soul to call. She had lots of casual acquaintances, girls she knew well enough to talk to when chance threw them together, to walk with down the halls at school, or eat with in the cafeteria. Unlike her sister Tobey, who had a large circle of fairly intimate friends, Midge was the type of person who became close friends with only one girl. That girl had been Judy. And now she was gone. Midge couldn't just call up Betty Fairless or

Mary Jean Crane or Eileen Clark. Mary Jean and Betty were no doubt doing something together. And Eileen would be with her friend Kathie Wade. It seemed to Midge suddenly that all the world was made up of twosomes, with only her left out. But that was a morbid idea and she dismissed it impatiently. Of course she'd make another friend when school started. And that would only be tomorrow. There might be some new girls, or someone she just hadn't thought of. All she had to do was get through the rest of today.

She jumped up and said, "I guess I'll take a walk past Bob's house—see if he's around." A little smile lifted the corners of her lips. "He's probably working on his car."

That was exactly what he was doing, she discovered a few minutes later. The lanky figure in faded jeans and oil-smudged T shirt squatted in front of the high, old-fashioned vehicle on the Piersons' drive, patiently polishing the brass casing of a headlight.

"Hi," Midge greeted and he looked up, a grin lighting his square, pleasant face below the bristling haircut.

"Hi yourself. What are you doing around loose? Where's Judy?"

It took Midge the better part of an hour to supply him with all the details. In the meantime Bob handed her another rag, indicated the can of polish, and put her to work on the other headlight. She didn't really mind, although she'd probably ruin her fingernails. Keeping busy might help to make time pass more quickly.

20

As they talked, Midge reflected that there was something nice and sexless about her relationship with Bob that made it sort of restful. No need to worry about what she said, or how she looked, or whether she made the right impression. Maybe this was the way she'd have felt about a brother, if she had had one. Midge sighed. The idea of having a brother had always appealed to her. Sisters were all right, of course, although things had sometimes been a bit hectic when they had all been at home. But, by the same token, it was mighty calm and quiet now that they were married. Janet lived away off in California, Tobey was hundreds of miles away at the university where her husband, Brose, was an instructor. Only Alicia was left in Edgewood and she was all wound up in her doctor husband, Adam, and their new baby. Midge sighed again.

"I might as well be an only child, like you!" she complained.

Bob chuckled. "Oh, it's not so bad. You get used to it."

"You do?" Midge sounded doubtful.

"Sure," Bob told her. "There are even some advantages. You get more attention from your parents, there aren't as many personality clashes as develop in a big family, you never have to wear hand-me-downs some older brother outgrew. On the other hand," he admitted, "you do get a little lonesome around home for somebody near your age to talk to."

"That's why I'll miss Judy so," Midge said. "We loved to talk to each other."

"You've still got me," Bob kidded.

Midge smiled, appreciating his effort to cheer her. "But there are things girls just can't talk about with boys."

"Like what, for instance?"

"Clothes," Midge enumerated on her fingers, "dates, new ways to do your hair, boys——"

"Boys?" Bob repeated. "Why do you talk about us?"

"Don't boys talk about girls?"

"Not very often," Bob grunted. "Why should we?"

"We're such a fascinating subject," Midge said lightly.

"Oh, sure," Bob's tone was sarcastic. "But any number of things are more fascinating. Motors, for instance."

"Now, really!" Midge exclaimed. "You just think that because you're not very mature."

"I'm older than you. I'll be sixteen before——"

"Maturity," Midge interrupted, "is mental age. Everyone knows that girls are much more mature than boys, even when they're the same age."

"I don't know it," Bob said flatly. "You listen to girls talking the most absolute drivel and then hear the intelligent conversation that goes on among boys and I don't see how you can believe any such thing."

"What sort of intelligent conversation?" Midge demanded. "About football or basketball or motors?"

"Well, don't tell me that's not smarter than to talk about clothes and how to fix your hair and stuff like that."

They argued the question for quite a while before Midge stopped abruptly in her polishing, struck by a sudden suspicion. "Bob Pierson," she said darkly, "tell me the truth about something! Did you get me all involved in this heated discussion to take my mind off Judy?"

"Now why would I do a thing like that?" Bob asked.

Midge scowled at him and he stared back at her with a perfectly serious face. Then, at the same moment, they both exploded into laughter.

"You character!" Midge exclaimed. "I'll bet you just wanted to keep me around to get this headlight polished, too!"

She threw the cleaning rag at him and Bob caught it. "I'll buy you a malt for your pay if you'll wait till I get cleaned up a little."

"Why not?" Midge grinned.

He might make a pretty good brother after all.

CHAPTER 3

The Sophomore Mixer

The first days of school were, as usual, a confused scramble—a schedule to be worked out, conflicting subjects to choose between, books to buy, new teachers to adjust to, different classrooms to become at home in. Midge rushed about with hundreds of other students, trying to get her bearings and straighten out all the kinks in her particular program. And gradually order began to be achieved out of chaos.

She didn't have too much time to think about Judy, for which she was thankful. But the awareness of her loss was present even when her mind was on something else. Everything would have been much more interesting if she'd had Judy to compare notes with.

Everyone commiserated with her over the loss of her closest friend. The girls she knew best were extra-friendly. But somehow it didn't help much to have Mary Jean ask sympathetically, "How can you bear it? Honestly, I'd simply die if Betty had to move away."

Nor could she bring herself to tag along all the time with Eileen and Kathie, no matter how cordial they were.

"The trouble is," she told Bob ruefully one night when he had dropped over to get her help with an English assignment, "I always seem to make the odd number. There'll be two girls and I make three, or maybe four will be talking together and I make the fifth. Probably no one else even notices, but I'm developing a thing about it."

"You're taking it too hard," Bob said, with typical male condescension. "Somebody'll turn up before long and then there you'll be, all set again. There must be dozens of girls in a big school like Edgewood who would like to have you for a special friend. It just takes a little time to get together, that's all."

"I suppose so," Midge sighed and returned to trying to pound some of the basic rules of grammar into Bob's head.

But she wasn't convinced that it was going to be such a simple matter to fill Judy's place. And, as the golden fall days passed, Midge discovered that it was possible to be lonely even in the midst of a laughing crowd in the cafeteria, or walking down the hall with several other girls. Judy's letters didn't help a bit either. For, contrary to her grim expectations, Judy was having a ball.

She wrote Midge: "I don't know if it's just because I'm somebody new and different or what, but everyone's been wonderful to me at school. The girls are so nice, and I've become quite friendly with Karen Bergstrom, who sits next to me in Spanish. She lives fairly close, so we've been seeing a lot of each other after school too. And she has the cutest brother, Carl, who's a junior and on the Student Council. You'd flip over him, he's six feet tall! I've already had one date with him and we're going out again next Friday night——" and on and on in similar vein.

Of course Judy had no idea that Midge wasn't having a grand time too. No hint of this was permitted to creep into Midge's answers to Judy's letters. Instead Midge made them very bright and gay, filled with news of clubs and classes, with accounts of funny incidents, with up-to-the-minute reports on who was going steady and who had broken up. She wrote in considerable detail about the Sophomore Mixer, an informal combination party and dance held in the school gym each fall.

"Norm Hagen asked me to dance," she informed Judy. "You remember him from last year. He's tall and quite attractive in a very smooth way and he's on the basketball team."

It was easy enough not to add in her letter that Norm had asked her to dance only once. Nor did she mention that during the rest of the evening her partners had consisted of a short boy named Joe Garrett, whose cowlick was level with her nose, of old reliable Bob, who, although he wasn't very keen on dancing, had rescued her from the sidelines a few times, and of Hans Dietrich.

She wrote Judy all about Hans, partly just to fill out her letter, but partly, too, because the whole incident

26

seemed quite funny in retrospect, although Midge hadn't found it so amusing at the time.

Hans was an exchange student from Germany, blond, blue-eyed, several inches taller than Midge and with a lean, muscular build. He seemed a bit older than most of the other sophomores—seventeen at least, Midge imagined. His English was good, but strongly accented. Chemistry was the only class they shared and their encounters had been limited to a few experiments in which they had taken part and a casual, "Hi," when they met elsewhere.

Midge hadn't even been close enough to him to say, "Hi," at the Mixer. Then they were thrown together in one of the charades that made up part of the evening's entertainment. And after their performance was over, Hans rather shyly suggested that they have some punch and cookies at the refreshment table.

Feeling a little sorry for him, Midge agreed. He must be suffering some pangs of discomfort and conspicuousness, she felt sure. In the whole gymful of students, Hans was the only boy in a neat dark suit, a white shirt and necktie. All the others were wearing sport jackets, T shirts, slacks—much less formal attire.

As though he read her thoughts, Hans said, as he politely handed her a punch cup, "I am too dressed up for the occasion, am I not? But one learns such things only by experience. Next time I'll know better."

His rueful smile was rather touching. Midge heard herself saying comfortingly, "I don't see why it matters, really. How would you know that Mixers are so informal unless someone told you in advance?"

"You are kind," Hans said warmly. "I should have asked someone, I suppose, but the thought did not occur to me."

Midge asked, "Don't the people you're staying with have any teen-age children?"

"Unfortunately no," he said. "The Armstrongs have a daughter and a son in college. I think they took in a foreign student partly so that their house would not be so empty and lonely with their own children away."

He wasn't a bit hard to talk to, once you got used to his accent and rather stiltedly correct English. But before he and Midge had time to exchange more than a few sentences, the music started up and the dancing part of the evening began.

"May I have this dance?" Hans crooked his arm with Old-World courtesy. "It seems to be a waltz, and that I know how to do."

But apparently, Midge was soon to discover, the European waltz and the version current in America were two different things. Hans was graceful enough— almost too graceful. He whirled her around and around until Midge's head was spinning. She had never danced this way before and hot color rose to her cheeks, not only with exertion, but with the realization that everyone must be staring. Luckily there was a break in the music just then, long enough for her to regain her equilibrium. Midge was relieved when the orchestra struck up a newer tune, one with a pronounced beat.

"Now I am lost," Hans confessed unhappily. "I regret I cannot do your American rock and roll."

28

"That's all right," Midge said, trying to keep her feelings from sounding in her tone. "I don't mind, really."

"Can we sit down and just talk?" Hans suggested.

"Of course."

But as they skirted the edge of the crowded floor on their way to the benches, a boy Midge knew only as Al turned away from the refreshment table, bearing two full cups of punch, and ran squarely into Hans. "Ooops, sorry," he apologized, looking chagrined at the spreading crimson stain on Hans's shirt.

"My fault," Han's tone was polite, but pained.

Al set down his now half-empty punch cups and tried to undo the damage with a couple of paper napkins. But the sticky stain was stubborn. "Gee, you look as if you've been shot," Al said with a weak grin. "I am sorry."

Hans managed a grin too. "It's all right. Please don't trouble yourself."

But when Al had gone on, Hans asked Midge apologetically, "Will you be so kind as to excuse me? I cannot stay like this. Anyway," his blue glance was rueful, "the music would probably be mostly for dances I don't know how to do yet." His tone, it seemed to Midge, underlined that last word slightly.

"I'm sorry you have to go," she told him. "But I do understand. And I enjoyed our dance." Under the circumstances that small white lie seemed not only justified but necessary.

"So did I," Hans said. "Good night."

The incident filled a whole page in her letter to

Judy. And Midge was grateful for that, since she actually didn't have too much to write about. Oh, she was busy enough, but not with the sort of things that made good letter material. There was school, and homework, and the extra household responsibilities she had had to assume due to the fact that her mother had broken her arm several weeks previously and it was still in a cast. And occasionally she sat with Alicia's and Adam's baby in order to give them a much-appreciated night out. On two Fridays in a row Bob asked her to go to the movies. The first time Midge accepted, but the second offer she declined with a rather vague excuse.

"What's the matter?" Bob asked. "You want to stay home and brood?"

"I'm not brooding!" Midge denied. "Quit saying that!"

"Then what are you going to do?"

"Well—I have to wash my hair. It's a mess. And there's that theme for English."

"Oh, come on now!" Bob said. "This is Friday! You've got the whole weekend to wash your hair and do themes."

"All right," Midge said, cornered. "If you want to know the truth, I'm not going with you because you know how it is at school. If we're seen together too often, word will get around that we're going steady. And then no one else will ask me for a date. Now are you satisfied?"

Bob stared at her blankly for a moment. Then a wide grin spread across his face. "Well, I'll be darned!"

"What's so funny?" Midge demanded with dignity. When Bob just continued to stand there, grinning that idiotic grin, she went on, "It's all very well for boys. You've got things all your own way. You can ask anyone you please for a date—provided, that is, she isn't all tied up with someone else. But a girl has to be careful about giving a wrong impression."

"I'll be darned!" Bob said again. He added, his tone growing thoughtful, "Maybe we should."

"Should what?" Midge demanded.

"Go steady, the way you said."

"Now you're being ridiculous," Midge told him icily. "I think the very idea of going steady is silly! You know that!"

"I think so too," Bob agreed. "But if things have reached the stage where you can't take a girl to the movies a few times—especially a girl you've known practically forever—without people getting crazy ideas —well," he wound up, "things have reached a pretty fantastic stage, that's all I've got to say!"

He sounded so deadly serious that Midge couldn't keep from laughing. "It is fantastic," she nodded. "But you know that's the way it is at school."

"Then I think something drastic should be done about it," Bob announced. "Why, it's positively un-American! How can we have life, liberty, and the pursuit of happiness if we——"

"What," Midge broke in, "would you suggest doing?"

"Let's defy the system," Bob said. "Let's go out together when we happen to feel like it, or, when we feel like going out with other people, let's do that."

"It sounds fine in theory," Midge's tone was regretful. "And I suppose it would be okay for you. Some boys do play the field. But mostly they'd just figure they shouldn't ask me for a date, because I must be your girl or I wouldn't be going out with you. So there I'd be half the time, sitting home."

"You'll be sitting home tonight," Bob pointed out, "if you don't go to the movies with me."

"True," Midge said, "but you have to look at these things with a broad perspective."

"I've got another idea," Bob grinned. "The movie doesn't sound too hot anyway. So how about if I just come over to your house and spend the evening? Then nobody but your folks would know. And you could make some fudge and I'd beat you at Scrabble—or maybe your parents would play some bridge with us."

Midge smiled back at him. It sounded like lots more fun than washing her hair and starting an English theme. "It's a date," she told Bob.

"Good." He patted his pocket appreciatively. "And just think of all the money I'll be saving, too."

CHAPTER 4

A New Friend

The following week was notable for Midge on two counts. First, Tom Brooks finally wrote. It wasn't much of a letter, actually, just a scrawled page telling about his trip home and about school and mentioning that he missed their long talks and all the fun they'd had at the lake. Tom wasn't nearly so fluent on paper as in person. Still, Midge treasured the letter, looking on it as the first link in a chain that would hold Tom and her together during their months of separation. And, of course, she lost no time in letting Judy know that Tom had written.

The second occurrence that made the week special was at once a source of pride and embarrassment to Midge. But it was its aftermath that was purely wonderful. She had duly composed her English theme and handed it in on Monday morning. On Thursday, when Miss Bates returned the graded papers, she had asked Midge's permission to read her essay, entitled "Conformity," to the class. Midge had sat twisting her pencil and squirming inwardly while the teacher's rich voice gave full value to the words she had written.

When she had finished, Miss Bates looked up, her pleased glance seeking Midge out as she announced, "This is the sort of fine, thoughtful work that makes a teacher feel her efforts are worth while. Thank you, Marjorie, for letting us all share this."

Midge had flushed with embarrassment; still, she felt proud and happy too. All during the rest of the period she experienced a warm glow. And later, when the bell had rung and she was on her way out, several classmates paused to congratulate her.

Then a girl's voice said just behind her, "I wish I could write like that. It was really good, Midge."

"Why, thanks." Midge turned, smiling, to see who had spoken. To her utter astonishment, it was Sandra Towers.

She was wearing one of her almost inevitable cashmere sweaters with a dyed-to-match skirt in a soft shade of rust that made her hair look even darker and brought out golden glints in her lovely brown eyes. Sandra was one of the most attractive and popular girls in the sophomore class. She was the undisputed leader of an ultra-smooth clique that included the most sought-after girls, the boys who were on the athletic teams or were the heads of important school clubs. Midge had long admired her from afar, but she couldn't recall ever having spoken more than half a dozen words with Sandra in her life.

Now, to her delighted surprise, Sandra's long, perfectly manicured fingers rested approvingly for a moment on her shoulder, Sandra's smile flashed dazzlingly and, without Midge's being quite sure how such a wonderful thing had happened, she found herself walking down the corridor with Sandra, talking as easily as though they were old friends.

As she wrote Judy that evening: "It turned out our lockers are fairly near each other, so we walked all the way there together. And she's so nice, Judy—not a bit snobbish or high-hat, as some of the kids think. You can't imagine how easy she is to talk with, how interested in what you're saying. And do you know what she told me? She said she'd noticed me a lot this year and thought I'd become ever so much sharper and more on-the-ball. In fact, she said she'd like for us to get to know each other better. And then she invited me over to her house tomorrow after school to listen to some new jazz records she's crazy about. So, of course, I'm planning to go. Isn't it exciting?"

Actually it turned out to be even more fun than Midge had anticipated. She hadn't realized that Sandra didn't live within walking distance of school. But when Midge asked, "How do we get there, take the school bus?" Sandra shook her head and said airily, "Don't be silly. I can't stand the bus. Pax will take us."

Pax, it developed, was none other than Hoyt Paxton, a junior and one of the school's outstanding track stars. Midge felt clutched just riding in his old, but impressive, convertible, even with Sandra sitting between them. Pax lived near Sandra in the exclusive new

35

country-club section, an area of winding roads, broad, landscaped lawns, and strikingly modern houses. He and Sandra seemed to be on the friendliest of terms, although after he had let them out and had driven on, she told Midge, "He's horrible, but his car comes in handy!"

"Why is he horrible?" Midge asked wonderingly, as she followed Sandra up the drive toward the Towerses' impressive white-brick and glass house.

"He bores me," the other girl said lightly. "Men with muscles usually do. But they're always the wheels around school, so we have to be sweet to them, don't we?" She smiled an irresistibly conspiratorial smile across her shoulder.

"Oh, sure," Midge heard herself agreeing. Then, as Sandra opened the front door and they stepped into a stone-paved entrance hall, Midge said, "Gee, your home is beautiful."

"Thanks," Sandra lightly dismissed the tasteful elegance of muted cocoa-brown walls and deep-piled off-white carpeting, of modern furniture and striking accessories that made all Midge could see of her surroundings look like a color page out of a decorating magazine.

A door at the back of the hall opened and a dour-faced angular woman glanced at them. "It's you," she said, and then disappeared with no further word of greeting.

"That's Agnes," Sandra told Midge, "the housekeeper. Her husband's the gardener and handy man. They live in the wing back of the garage."

36

"Oh?" Midge said a trifle blankly. The only other person she knew who had a housekeeper was Miss Tess Wentworth. And Miss Tess's housekeeper was plump and cheerful and almost as old as Miss Tess herself, a different breed entirely than Agnes seemed to be. "Is she always so—impersonal?" Midge queried.

Sandra's smile was Mona Lisa-ish. "We understand each other, Agnes and I. She leaves me absolutely alone and vice versa. That's the way we both like it. My room's over here."

She led Midge along a carpeted hallway and pushed open a door halfway along it. "Welcome to my castle."

There was something almost unreal, or at least theatrical, about such perfection. The room was done in coral and white, with touches of black for contrast. It, too, was deeply carpeted, and the windows were hung with silken drapes in an abstract design. There were twin beds with wrought-iron headboards and one whole wall of closets. Another wall held bookshelves, devoted mainly to striking and expensive-looking bric-a-brac, and a built-in record player and television set. Through an open doorway Midge glimpsed a perfectly appointed bath in matching tones.

"It's lovely," she breathed softly, "just lovely." Until this moment she had always thought her own bedroom fairly adequate. Now the first small seed of discontent was sown. The Towerses must be very rich, she decided, very rich indeed!

Midge spent the next couple of hours most enjoyably. She and Sandra talked and listened to records, of which Sandra had a terrific collection. Midge helped Sandra with an English assignment which had puzzled her and they drank Cokes and ate cookies which Sandra brought in from the kitchen. By the time Midge felt she should leave, they were much better acquainted and any slight stiffness or strangeness which had existed between them at first had been dissipated. Midge had learned that Sandra's father was a consulting engineer, whose job entailed a great deal of travel. Her mother—a strikingly beautiful woman, according to the photograph Sandra showed Midge—was a successful career woman, head of the advertising department of Wentworth's, Edgewood's largest department store.

When Sandra mentioned this, Midge couldn't resist telling her that Mr. Wentworth, who owned the store, was the father of her brother-in-law, Adam. "What my father calls a shirttail relation," she added, smiling. "I know Miss Tess Wentworth real well, too. She's such a sweet old lady."

"Really?" Sandra said. "I don't like to be around old people. They depress me."

"Miss Tess wouldn't," Midge said. "She's fun to talk to. And she has an attic full of the most absolutely fabulous clothes you ever saw—ball gowns she wore as a young girl, lovely old furs, velvet bonnets with ostrich plumes."

Sandra listened politely, but obviously was not impressed. "They must be full of moths and dust by this time and smell all moldy."

"No they don't," Midge denied. "They're very carefully put away. My sister Tobey borrowed some stuff one time for a party or a play at school and they were just gorgeous."

Sandra wandered over to the window and stared out at the western sky, washed with opalescent pink by the setting sun. "My mother should be home pretty soon, I think. Why don't you stay for dinner and meet her?"

"Oh, I really can't, thanks," Midge said. After all, this was the first time she'd ever set foot in Sandra's house. No point in wearing out her welcome, especially when she would so love to be invited back again. "My folks are expecting me. I should actually leave right away and get home in time to help Mom with dinner. She broke her arm a while ago and even now that she has the cast off, it's still sort of stiff."

"That's too bad," Sandra said politely, still staring out at the sunset.

"I was wondering—" Midge hesitated, "how I'll get home? It's pretty far from here."

"Oh, I'm sorry," Sandra turned. "I'll take you."

"I didn't realize you were old enough to drive."

"Well—I'm not quite," Sandra admitted, smiling. "I won't be sixteen for another month. In the meantime, what's the difference, so long as I obey all the laws and don't get caught? I've been driving without a license for ages."

Midge didn't feel too happy about the situation; still, she had little choice but to follow Sandra out to the garage. It was the largest one Midge had seen, and there were two cars in it, a station wagon and a little cream-colored MG. "Mother has the Cad," Sandra said casually. "This one's mine. Hop in," she indicated the MG. "It's really for my birthday, but Dad gave me the keys this summer."

"He knows you drive, then."

"Of course." Sandra backed the little car expertly out of the garage and down the long drive. "Living away out here, how else would I get around? I have to use some discretion about where I go. I can't drive to school, for instance. Too many people there know my age. But almost anyplace else is okay, if I'm careful."

She covered the two-mile drive to the Heydons' house with exemplary precision. As Midge got out of the car, she told Sandra, "It was lots of fun. Will you come over and see me soon?"

"Why not?" Sandra smiled. "I enjoyed it too."

"And thanks for bringing me home."

"That's okay. See you." Sandra was off through the deepening blue dusk with a wave.

Walking up the steps, Midge hoped that Mrs. Towers would be home by the time Sandra got there. It would be grim to come in a second time to Agnes' supremely disinterested, "It's you."

"Hi," Midge called from the hallway. "I'm home."

"Good," came Mom's voice from the kitchen. "You're just in time to set the table."

"You mean you got dinner all by yourself?"

The kitchen looked warm and cozy with its crisp yellow curtains and pale-gray walls. True, it was pretty old-fashioned compared with the miraculously equipped room presided over by the unappreciative

40

Agnes. But it smelled good, with the fragrance of pork roasting. And Mom's pleasant features wore a customary smile as she answered, "My arm hardly bothers me a bit any more."

Midge slid her schoolbooks onto a chair. "I," she informed her mother, "have been seeing how the other half lives." And, as she busied herself with dishes and silver, she proceeded to describe the Towerses' house glowingly, especially Sandra's incredible room with its lovely furnishings and that solid wall of closets. "Imagine," Midge sighed, "having that many clothes!"

"It must be wonderful," Mom agreed. She asked then, as she measured coffee into the percolator, "Was her mother nice?"

"I didn't meet her," Midge said. "She works. And Sandra's father's hardly ever home. He travels a lot on his job. There's a housekeeper, but she's awfully grouchy. Sandra doesn't seem to mind, though. I guess she's used to it, but—I don't know. I should think it would be terribly lonesome for her. Still, to get to live in a place like that . . . have your own car . . ." her voice trailed off.

She wasn't quite sure whether she felt envy or pity for Sandra. Her reactions to the circumstances of the other girl's life were decidedly mixed. One thing Midge was sure of, though. She had liked Sandra, enjoyed being with her. If the feeling were mutual, there seemed to be no reason they couldn't become good friends.

CHAPTER 5

First Date

"Hey, wait for me!" Bob Pierson's call stopped Midge as she was heading homeward after school. Yellow leaves lay in a bright drift across the sidewalk and there was a crisp freshness in the early October air. Midge stirred the leaves idly with one foot, waiting for Bob.

"How come you're walking?" he demanded as they fell into step, his sweater-clad arm bumping hers in shifting his books from one side to the other.

"What do you mean?" Midge asked. "I usually walk."

"Not lately." Bob shook his head. "You're always riding off with Sandra Towers or Hoyt Paxton or some of that crowd."

Midge bristled at the tone in which he said the final two words. "Is there anything wrong with that?"

"Depends on the kind of people you like, I suppose."

"Watch it," Midge smiled. "Your sour grapes are showing."

"Sour grapes!" Bob snorted. "You really think I care a hoot about that bunch of would-be wheels and small-time big shots?"

"Maybe not," Midge said. "Everyone to his own taste. But whether you care about them or not, you haven't any right to imply that they aren't some of the most important people at school. Sandra's terrifically popular, and so are Debbie Burke and Sharon Cutler. And as for Pax and Norm Hagen and the other boys—well, you're just being childish to say they're not really outstanding. Everyone knows they are!"

"You used to think they were a bunch of snobs too," Bob said aggrievedly. "You could see through all their airs and pretenses. Now, just because Sandra's condescended to take you up——"

"She hasn't taken me up," Midge broke in hotly. "We've become friends. Is that so hard to understand?"

"I can't see what you have in common," Bob argued. "Friends have got to have similar interests, the same ideas about life, some agreement as to what's important and what isn't. You can't tell me you see eye to eye with someone like her."

"Why not?" Midge demanded. She couldn't help adding, "But I really don't see how it concerns you."

"Somebody's got to try to straighten you out," Bob growled. "You can't have ideas like hers because she's the type who figures since she's got expensive clothes and a swell house and a fancy car of her own, she's got

43

it made. She considers all those things vitally important. You know better than that; you've got a sounder sense of values."

"If Sandra were like that—which she isn't!—why do you think she'd bother with me?" Midge asked logically.

"You must have something she wants." Bob's tone was sour. "I'm not sure what, but there's got to be some such reason."

"You're just impossible," Midge said. "I don't know why I even waste time talking to you."

"Because we're old friends," Bob told her. "And no matter how you fight against it, you know I've got your best interests at heart. That's why I'm talking this way to you."

"Gee, thanks," Midge drawled. "Now that you've given me the benefit of your advice, let's drop it, shall we?"

"You just won't listen to reason," Bob accused. "That bunch has got you so dazzled you can't see them for what they are."

"Oh, honestly!" Midge said. "I'm not even listening!"

Bob was entirely mistaken. She wasn't dazzled, although new color and excitement had seemed to spark her life almost from the beginning of her association with Sandra. Their friendship had developed quickly, and Sandra's favor had carried with it acceptance by a whole new circle of acquaintances. Sophomore wheels who had scarcely been aware of Midge's existence were now on gratifyingly friendly terms with her. Naturally she was delighted with this new recognition and importance. But she was not dazzled!

"Okay," Bob said. "Just don't say I didn't warn you."

"Oh, I won't," Midge assured him sweetly. "When they cast me aside like an old shoe, I'll remember this day and how you tried so hard to make me see things in their true light. I'll even give you permission to say, 'I told you so.' "

"Very funny," Bob scowled. "How about going to the movies with me tonight?"

"I'm sorry," Midge's words were polite but her tone didn't sound at all as though she meant it, "I can't."

"Why not? It's Friday."

"I know what day it is."

"Still afraid somebody'll think we're going steady?"

Midge shook her head. "It just so happens I have another date." She could tell Bob was getting ready to ask who it was with, so she forestalled him by adding, "Sandra and Rick Lewis and Norm and I are doubling."

"She fix it up for you with Norm?" Bob asked nastily.

"That," Midge blazed, "is none of your business!"

Luckily they were practically at her front walk, so she was able to turn on her heel and march briskly away, leaving Bob staring rather uncertainly after her. She didn't even say good-by, so hot and choking was the anger that flared up within her. Maybe, she realized, she wouldn't have felt so furious if his suspicion hadn't happened to be true. . . .

Midge came downstairs to dinner with her hair still up in bobby pins and wearing her plaid gingham duster. She had shampooed and bathed and done her nails fastidiously. Not until later would she don the white sweater and soft green pleated skirt which she had finally decided to wear.

"Are you on your way to haunt a house?" her father inquired in his usual facetious tone. "Or is this just something new in the way of dinner dress?"

"Now, Henry," Mom said, smiling, "don't tease. She has an important date."

"A dance?" Dad asked. "I wasn't approached about a new formal. You two must be slipping."

"Not a dance," Midge shook her head. "We're only going to the movies."

"It's the boy she's going with who's important," Mom explained, "not where they're going. This is her first date with him."

"Who is he?" Dad asked interestedly. Then, when Midge had mentioned his name, he queried, "And just why is Norm Hagen so special that he rates all these preliminaries?"

Ordinarily Midge didn't mind her father's kidding. He had a tremendous sense of humor and, although his jokes were sometimes a bit corny, she was so used to him that she usually could take this sort of thing in stride. Tonight, however, she felt quick color rush to her face and something hatefully close to tears pressing hard at her eyelids. The thing to do, she knew, was kid right back with him. But she could only man-

46

age to gulp, "He's a wheel at school—on the basketball team——"

Whatever else he might be, Dad was not insensitive. He noted the danger signals and retreated in good order. "I see," he nodded. "I'll be interested to meet him." Being Dad, he couldn't resist adding, "Provided, that is, I can see him without standing on a chair. Most of these basketball players seem seven feet tall."

In the laughter that followed, Midge felt a loosening of the inexplicable tension that had gripped her. She couldn't imagine why she'd got all choked up over nothing at all.

The rest of the meal passed agreeably, as usual. Over dessert Dad remarked, "We had a German exchange student as our speaker at the Rotary luncheon this week."

"Oh? Was he interesting?" Mom asked.

"Very," Dad nodded. "He talked mostly about the differences between the European school system and ours. Seems they go in for a lot less frills and extras and stick closer to basic education. But I got the idea he liked it over here."

"Was he tall and sort of blond?" Midge asked. "Was it Hans Dietrich?" Then, at her father's nod, she added, "He's in my Chemistry class." The memory of their wild dance at the Mixer washed over her and she smiled, sharing the experience with her parents, right up to the climax of the spilled punch.

"Poor boy," Mom said with quick sympathy, "he must have been terribly embarrassed."

47

"I guess so," Midge agreed. "He's hardly more than said 'Hi' to me since."

Dad remarked that after Hans's talk was finished a lot of them had questioned him concerning his impressions of America and what he liked, or didn't like, about it. "He was quite frank as to what he liked," Dad chuckled, "but we had to pin him down to get him to mention what he considered our failings."

"He probably thought it would be rude to eat your lunch and then tear you down right to your faces," Mom said. "What did he like best about us?"

"Our freedoms that we take so much for granted," Dad said, "and our breezy ways and friendliness."

"And what didn't he like?" Midge asked curiously.

"Under considerable pressure he admitted that he felt Americans as a whole were too materialistic, too prone to measure a person's success by his earnings, rather than by the kind of man he was, the life he led. Then we got really personal and asked him to go beyond generalities and tell us what he himself found most distasteful about life right here in Edgewood."

"And what did he say?" Midge and Mom asked in unison.

"He said," Dad told them, "that the thing he personally found most annoying was the fact that American girls appear incapable of walking. It seems not having a car at his disposal is an almost insurmountable obstacle to dating. In Germany, he told us, you could invite a girl to go for a walk, but in Edgewood such a thing was unheard of. Of course this got a big laugh at Rotary, but I felt a little sorry for the poor guy myself."

"Is that really true?" Mom asked, and Midge felt both her parents' glances as they waited for her answer.

"Well—" she had to admit ruefully, "in a way I suppose it is. I mean, of course we can walk—in fact I like to myself—but a walk doesn't exactly seem like a real date."

That final word brought her thoughts back to the present with a jerk. "Oh gee," she said, jumping up, "I've got to rush! Norm's coming for me at eight. Mom, do you mind if I don't help with the dishes tonight?"

"Of course not," her mother assured her. "Go ahead."

"But you've got an hour," Dad called after her, as she headed for her room at a run. "Don't panic."

Midge's hair, as was almost inevitable on important occasions, gave her some trouble. She finally had it arranged to her liking and was trying to decide whether to wear her pearls or the gold chain with the jade-green pendant when she heard a car pull up on the drive. It couldn't be eight yet, she thought, her fingers fumbling nervously with the clasp of her pearls. But a look at her dresser clock indicated that it was. In fact it was five minutes after. Midge drew a deep, deep breath and closed her eyes, then opened them for a final appraising glance at her reflection in the mirror. She was halfway down the stairs by the time the bell rang. She opened the door and Norm stood there, tall and unbelievably attractive in a tweed sport jacket and dark slacks, his brown hair gleaming under the porch light.

"Hi," he said, smiling. "All ready?"

"As soon as I get my coat," Midge told him. "Come on in a minute and meet my parents."

"We haven't much time," Norm warned, "if we want to catch the start of the picture. And Sandra and Rick are out in the car." Still, he stepped into the hall and helped Midge on wtih the jacket she took from the closet.

Her mother and father came as far as the living-room doorway and Midge murmured introductions. Her parents were pleasant, Norm punctiliously polite despite his obvious impatience to be off. When he and Midge were out on the porch with the door closed behind them, she could clearly hear his sigh of relief.

"Glad that's over," he said, slipping his hand under her elbow as they went down the steps. "First time I date a girl I always feel as if her old man's going to ask for my credentials or something. At least yours spared me the bit about driving carefully."

Midge laughed with him, a heady sense of excitement swelling within her. "You're just lucky," she told Norm. "He sometimes does say that."

Also, she thought, he often told her not to stay out too late. But tonight she and Norm had been spared both those indignities. Midge felt grateful to her father for being so considerate. Was it possible, she wondered, that he finally realized she was growing up?

CHAPTER 6

Advice from Sandra

Although Midge could scarcely bear to admit it even to herself, her date with Norm proved a bit disappointing. Oh, he was pleasant enough, and maybe it was merely her own lack of ease that made her feel as if they finished the evening without knowing each other much better than they had at its start. Norm's hand pressed hers a couple of times while they were watching the movie, but although Midge's heart raced at his touch, there really didn't seem to be anything very personal about the contact. It was as though, she thought, Norm felt that when you took a girl to a show, she expected you to hold her hand and that he was simply doing the customary thing under the circumstances.

Afterward they drove out to the Lazy-M, a soda and hamburger place a few miles from Edgewood, much frequented by the young crowd. Midge saw several people she knew sitting on stools at the long counter or in booths around the knotty-pine walls. And the looks sent her way gave her a sense of pride in being with Norm and Sandra and Rick. True, both boys actually seemed to pay more attention to Sandra than to her, but for this Midge couldn't blame them. Sandra was so lovely, so effervescent, so full of fun and conversation that Midge felt her own personality almost blotted out by that of the other girl.

Still, as Rick drove them home, Sandra's head rested cozily on his shoulder and Midge was acutely conscious of Norm's arm curved along the back of the seat behind her. And while Sandra and Rick embraced in the car on the Heydons' drive, Norm walked with Midge up the steps and across the porch, their clasped hands swinging between them. Midge's heart fluttered. What came next?

"I had a wonderful time," she told Norm, her voice not sounding quite natural. "Thanks."

"So did I," Norm answered. He gave her shoulders a tentative hug and looked down questioningly into her face. After a moment his grip loosened and he said, "See you. G'night," and left.

Midge stood in the hallway, just inside the closed door, until she heard the sound of Rick's car pulling away. She felt, but wasn't entirely sure, that Norm had been going to kiss her—or at least try to—but then had thought better of it. Why, she wondered? Had her face failed to offer the invitation he expected? And if he had tried to kiss her, would she have let him?

Uncertainty swelled in Midge. She didn't feel very sure of anything at the moment. She really hadn't wanted to be kissed by Norm and yet, since he hadn't made the attempt, she felt vaguely disappointed. Maybe, she told herself, as she switched off the hall light and went quietly up the stairs, she'd understand her mixed reactions better when she'd had time to sleep on the matter and acquire some perspective. . . .

Midge had promised to baby-sit with little Anne the following afternoon, so that Alicia could go to a bridge luncheon. She had just given the baby her two-o'clock bottle and settled her in her pink crib for a nap when the doorbell rang. To Midge's surprise, it was Sandra.

"Well, hi," Midge beamed, throwing the door wide.

"I stopped at your house and your mother said you were here." Sandra came in, looking beautifully smart in skin-tight black pants and a madly striped Italian sweater, her dark hair becomingly tousled by the wind. Out at the curb, Midge glimpsed the cream-colored MG. "You don't mind my tracking you down?"

"Of course not," Midge waved her to a chair in Alicia's attractively Mid-Victorian living room. "Glad to have company. The baby's just about asleep."

"How come you're stuck with her?" Sandra asked. "Do they take advantage of you like this very often?"

"I don't mind," Midge said. "It's only a Saturday afternoon and I wasn't doing anything special anyway."

Sandra shrugged. "It's your business, of course. But that sort of thing's insidious. I'd put my foot down right at the start." She asked then, "How did you enjoy last night?"

53

"It was lots of fun."

"You and Norm hit it off all right, didn't you?"

"I—think so," Midge said. "Of course, I'm not sure how he felt about me."

"He didn't linger very long on your doorstep," Sandra drawled. "He was back in the car before Rick and I expected him. Didn't you even let him kiss you good night?"

"He didn't try," Midge admitted, feeling her face grow warm. "If he had, I'm not sure I'd have let him."

"Probably he could tell that from your manner," Sandra said shrewdly, "which was why he didn't stick his neck out."

"But it was only a first date," Midge objected.

"If a boy gets the idea you just don't like him at all," Sandra told her, "he won't ask for a second one."

"But I can like him without wanting to kiss him so soon," Midge argued. "I'm sure I didn't act as if I didn't like him."

Sandra sighed. "You're pretty naïve in some ways. We'll have to get you over that."

"I don't think I'm naïve," Midge said stubbornly, "just because I don't like the idea of kissing every boy I go out with. That's pretty promiscuous, it seems to me."

"My, what big words you use," Sandra's smile was teasing. "What's so important about a little kiss? It doesn't mean any more than—oh, a handshake. It's just a way of letting a boy know you enjoyed his company, that you appreciated his spending his money on you. Didn't you want Norm to know that?"

54

Midge frowned. She didn't like to disagree with Sandra, or do anything that might affect their friendship, which she valued so highly. On the other hand, you had to speak up and state your own opinion. If a relationship couldn't stand truthfulness, it was worth nothing.

She said slowly, "I think a kiss means more than a handshake. Or else—well, what's the point in it at all? If a person just goes around kissing everybody she had a pleasant evening with—then, when she really finds someone she likes a lot, how's she going to express her liking?"

"There are kisses—and kisses!" Sandra said meaningfully. "You'll find out." She laughed then, adding, "Even if you are naïve, you're cute. You've just got a lot to learn, that's all. But I'm a good teacher."

Her laughter was contagious. Midge felt her own seriousness being dissipated by Sandra's airy manner, even though she was by no means convinced she could ever entirely agree with the other girl's ideas. But that didn't mean they couldn't be good friends. That had been a silly, unreasonable idea of Bob's that friends had to share the same viewpoint, see eye to eye on everything. Such unfailing agreement would make for a dull, static relationship. It was more fun this way. And there was no reason for her to be brought around to Sandra's way of thinking. Maybe she could bring Sandra around to hers.

Midge said, her tone as light as Sandra's, "I'm not sure I'll make a very good student. But anyway——" she left it at that.

"Anyway," Sandra picked it up, "there's no reason we have to concentrate on Norm Hagen. Next time we'll make it someone else. You don't want the idea to get around that you're going steady."

"Gee, no," Midge agreed. "I think that's the height of stupidity. Unless, that is, you're older and really serious."

Sandra nodded. "I'm with you there. Going steady gets very dull. I wonder who ever started the silly business anyway."

"Have you gone steady?" Midge asked interestedly. "I know you aren't now, but did you ever?"

A faint smile pulled at the corners of Sandra's lips. "For several months last year I went steady with Terry Blaine. Terry the Brain, I used to call him when I wanted to make him mad."

Midge knew Terry only slightly. He was an attractive, rather serious junior, a member of the Student Council and on the staff of the school paper. She could remember having seen Sandra and him together a great deal last spring. Now they apparently had nothing whatever to do with each other. Midge couldn't help being a little curious as to what had happened. But she thought it would be rather prying to come right out and ask.

However, Sandra seemed to be in a reminiscent, confiding mood. She went on, her dark gaze fixed on space, "That was around the same time, you may recall, that I was very good friends with Tricia Farnham. You know her."

56

"She's in my Math class," Midge nodded, "but I don't know her very well."

Suddenly she was aware that Sandra's gaze was turned questioningly toward her, seemed to be pinning her down. "I saw you talking with her yesterday in the hall at school."

"She asked me about the assignment," Midge recalled.

"Oh," Sandra's smile was enigmatic. "I thought she might have been talking about me."

"She wasn't." Midge frowned. "Why should you think such a thing?"

Sandra shrugged. "It was just an idea. She's pretty bitter against me, I understand. Not that she has the slightest reason to be. If anyone should be sore, it's I."

"What happened?" Midge couldn't help asking. After all, Sandra herself had brought the whole matter up.

"I never knew such a jealous, resentful person," Sandra admitted. "She's dying to be popular and yet she doesn't have any idea how to go about it. I guess that's why she got friendly with me. She figured I could help her. But you know boys don't go for that brusque, independent type and I tried to tell her that. I used to get dates for her all the time too. But she never really appreciated it. All she wanted was to hang around and try to take all the most attractive boys away from me. Of course she didn't succeed, but things got a bit awkward sometimes."

"I can imagine," Midge said sympathetically. She

57

hadn't realized Tricia was like that. But then, she scarcely knew her.

"When I was going steady with Terry," Sandra went on, "she told him the most outrageous stories about me—actual lies! Then, when he and I broke up because he'd swallowed some of her tales, she tried to grab him on the rebound. They did go together for a short while, but it all blew up very quickly. I don't like to sound catty or anything, but if I were you, I'd have nothing whatever to do with her. She's such a strange girl. In a way I feel sorry for her, even after the way she treated me. She's so mixed up."

"I don't think you're catty," Midge said loyally. "It seems to me you're being very tolerant, under the circumstances. Thanks for warning me. I'll watch out for her."

The next time she encountered Tricia in Math, Midge couldn't help thinking of all Sandra had told her. Tricia had very clear blue eyes and a few freckles. Brown hair hugged her head closely and was cut in pixie bangs across her forehead. There was a sort of blunt forthrightness about her, just as Sandra had said, but her smile was warmly winning. Midge actually had to steel herself against it as Tricia hurried to catch up with her in the corridor after class.

"Hi," Tricia greeted. "You going to G.A.A. meeting?"

Such had been Midge's intention, although Sandra often kidded her about her interest in the organization. "Why, yes," she admitted. Then, searching desperately for an excuse not to go with Tricia, she added,

"But I've got an errand to do first and I'll have to stop at my locker."

"Oh," Tricia said on a slightly rising inflection. She added, "I'll probably see you there then," and hurried on, leaving Midge with the uncomfortable feeling that she had seen through the weak excuse.

But Midge did have an errand. She had to return a book to the library or pay an overdue fine. And she wanted to leave some stuff in her locker. So she hadn't really lied to Tricia. Still, the whole affair left her with an unpleasant taste in her mouth. She admitted to herself, "If it hadn't been for the things Sandra told me, I'd have gone to the meeting with her even if we did have to stop at the library on the way. I hate to snub anyone like that. And she seemed so friendly."

Still, Midge couldn't help wondering whether Tricia's overture might have had its roots in her dislike of Sandra, in a desire to repeat some of the outrageous tales Sandra had said she'd told before. If such were the case, it would be better not to get involved with her, not give her another chance to stir old misunderstandings and resentments.

Seeing some girls she knew entering the library, Midge hurried to join them. If they all went on to the G.A.A. meeting together, it would discourage Tricia from making another effort to seek her out.

CHAPTER 7

Sandra Gets Caught

Despite the fact that Mom was always pleasant in her attitude toward Sandra, Midge sensed, or at least suspected, that she didn't like her new friend too well. Since a climate of frankness had always existed between them, Midge finally came right out and asked her mother whether this were so.

"Dislike is too strong a word," Mom objected, pausing in the act of spreading frosting on a chocolate cake. "For one thing, I don't feel I know her very well. You go to her house a lot more often than she comes here, so I haven't actually been around her a great deal. Then, too," Mom smiled faintly, "she's one of those young people who set up a solid wall between themselves and the older generation. You don't do that. Judy never did, nor some of your other friends. But Sandra's the type who makes me feel very old, almost ready for discard."

60

"Why do you say that?" Midge asked. "She's always polite to you, isn't she?"

"Oh, very," Mom nodded. "But she's polite in the way one would be polite to a person who doesn't even speak the same language. It's as if there isn't any point of contact between us. And I think Sandra prefers it that way. I wonder if she's that detached with her own mother, simply because of the age difference?"

"You're not being entirely fair to her," Midge argued. "She's never around older people. That's probably why she doesn't care for them. She must love her parents, of course. But they're hardly ever home. She can't spend much time with them when her father travels and her mother's so involved with her job."

"I suppose not," Mom said. "But are you sure it's not her own choice to shut them out? What's her mother like, by the way?"

"Very glamorous," Midge told her. "Quite stunning. Of course I've only met her briefly a couple of times. She seems as disinterested in Sandra as Sandra is in her. And I've never even seen Mr. Towers in all the times I've been there."

"It must be a curious household."

"I suppose it is, in a way," Midge had to admit. "But their home is so beautiful and they give Sandra everything she wants. And Agnes is there to take care of things."

"They may give her every material thing she wants," Mom pointed out quietly, "but it certainly doesn't sound as though she gets much of their time, or interest, or personal attention."

"She doesn't seem to want that," Midge explained. "She says she'd simply die if she always had someone hovering around, asking questions and telling her what she should or shouldn't do."

"Does she consider we do that with you?" Mom asked, her expression quizzical.

Midge grinned at her. "I don't know. I don't care, really. I like the way I'm treated around here."

"Good," Mom nodded. "We don't want you leaving home."

"Wouldn't dream of it—at least, not until after I get to lick that frosting bowl."

"It's a deal."

But later, after Midge had eaten the remainder of the frosting and gone up to her room to do her homework, she found it hard to concentrate. She kept thinking about Sandra and the things Mom had said. Sandra's air of detachment toward her parents must have grown out of their initial rejection of her, Midge reflected loyally. Somewhere along the way they had shut a door on Sandra. Probably at first she had tried to open it, then grown weary of the effort. And gradually her bored disenchantment had broadened to include all older people.

It was a shame, really. The warm give-and-take relationship that existed between Midge and her parents made her realize how much Sandra was missing. But it had to be a two-way effort; Sandra couldn't achieve results alone. And if her parents declined to meet her halfway—well, Midge didn't know the answer to that. Sighing, she started on her Math assign-

62

ment. At least in Math everything was definite and certain. Each problem had a correct answer, which, with a reasonable amount of thought, one could arrive at. In this respect it was somewhat different from life —more simple, not nearly so confusing and complicated.

Almost an hour later, when Midge had just started downstairs to see about helping her mother with dinner, the phone rang. As soon as Midge said, "Hello?" Sandra began abruptly, "I'm in a mess! I was driving home from Sharon's and I went through a stop sign. It's so ridiculous! There wasn't another car in sight, but a stupid cop stopped me."

"And you don't have a license," Midge gasped.

"You'd think I'd committed murder, at least," Sandra said succinctly. "They took me to the crumby old station and called my mother. If they'd simply given me a ticket, we could have had it fixed. My father knows the right people. This way it's a Big Deal and Mother's furious. She'll have to pull all sorts of strings to straighten it out. We're going now to see a judge she knows."

"Is there anything I can do to help?" Midge asked.

Sandra's tone assumed a coaxing note. "You know that darned English theme that's due tomorrow?"

"Haven't you done that yet?" Midge exclaimed. Miss Bates had assigned it weeks ago.

"I haven't done it," Sandra said, "and now it doesn't look as if I'll get a chance to. This business with the judge may take hours. He'll have to give me a full-scale lecture, at least! Midge, won't you do a theme

63

for me? Not as good as your usual ones or old Bates might get suspicious. Just good enough to get me off the hook. Please?"

"Gee, Sandra—" Midge felt a queer, sinking sensation. She wanted to help, but this struck her as downright dishonest.

"If you type it," Sandra went on desperately, "she'll never know the difference. I always type stuff. Just don't make it too good."

"I don't like the idea a bit," Midge's tone was grave. If Sandra weren't in such a jam, she wouldn't even consider it.

"Just this once," Sandra murmured pleadingly. "I'll never ask you to again, I promise. You will do it, won't you?"

"I—guess so," Midge gulped. How could she refuse?

"Thanks a million," Sandra's tone was abjectly grateful, but relief sounded clearly in it. "I won't forget this. Now I've got to go. Wish me luck."

"Luck," Midge said. She replaced the receiver slowly.

"What was that all about?" Mom asked with natural curiosity from the kitchen doorway.

Midge explained about Sandra's predicament with the police. She didn't go into the matter of the English theme.

"You mean she's been driving all this time without a license?" Mom asked. "I just assumed she must be sixteen."

"She will be soon." Midge felt she had to offer something in the way of a mitigating excuse. But it sounded weak.

"Why would her parents let her do such a thing?" Mom frowned. "Or didn't they know?"

"They knew," Midge said. "Her car was supposed to be a birthday gift, but she's had the keys for months. I guess they just figured no one would know the difference, so it really didn't matter."

"You don't figure that way, though," Mom said.

"No," Midge had to admit. "I was pretty perturbed about it when I first found out. Then—well, I guess I just didn't give it much thought any more. But it's not right, of course. Still, I'm sorry she got caught."

Mom nodded. "I wonder what will happen?"

Midge shrugged. "The Towerses have connections, as the saying goes. Some judge is a friend of theirs. Sandra and her mother are going to see him tonight. He'll probably fix it all up."

"Now that I don't approve of," Mom said positively. "Even if such an attitude marks me as hopelessly square, I don't believe in wirepulling and using influence. It's wrong."

"I know," Midge agreed. "But there's nothing I can do about it." She asked then, "You need any help with dinner?"

"Not right now," Mom said. "You can set the table later."

Midge started slowly up the stairs. "I'll be down in a little while," she told her mother. "I've got an English theme to do. Maybe I can at least get started on it before dinner. . . ."

It didn't salve Midge's conscience to hear later on

that Miss Bates had given Sandra a B on the theme. But Sandra was jubilant. "It was perfect," she told Midge. "An A might have made her wonder. You'll never know how much I appreciate it."

"Just don't ever ask me to do it again," Midge warned unhappily, "because I won't."

The two girls, as had become their frequent custom, were doing their homework together. They sprawled comfortably in Sandra's luxurious bedroom, a stack of records filling the air with sound. But the noise in no way interfered with their studying or the conversation that punctuated it.

Now Sandra said, her smile quizzical, "What a New England conscience you have! Actually, why is it any worse to write a theme for me than to help me out with my assignments, as you always do?"

"It's altogether different," Midge insisted. "When we do our homework together, it involves mutual effort. I don't just do it all for both of us."

"But you're so smart," Sandra said, "you contribute a lot more to the mutual effort than I do."

"I'm no smarter than you," Midge denied.

"Ha! What about all those big fat A's you get?"

"You'd get A's, too, if you worked a little harder."

"That's the difference between us." Sandra stretched like a kitten and collapsed backward across the bed. "I'm just naturally lazy. Good grades are important to you, while I don't give a darn. All I want is to get by without flunking."

Midge said slowly, "It's not the grades that are so important to me. I—just like to learn all about things."

"You have what Miss Bates is always talking about in class," Sandra drawled teasingly, "intellectual curiosity. Now I'm curious enough, but not, I'm afraid, intellectually."

"Don't you want to go to college?" Midge queried. "The requirements are getting stiffer all the time, you know."

Sandra shrugged. "Just for the social side. Sorority life, proms—I'd hate to miss all that. So I expect I'll stir myself later on enough to squeak in somewhere. Who knows, maybe some of your intellectual curiosity may even rub off on me."

She was a strange girl. Sometimes, despite their close association, Midge felt she didn't know her at all. Whether this was due to the fact that Sandra kept the core of herself secret and shut away, or simply that many of the other girl's attitudes and reactions were so inexplicably different from her own, Midge wasn't quite sure.

Sandra had managed to get out of her difficulties over the lack of a driver's license with no more punishment than a stern warning. However, her parents had issued an ultimatum forbidding her to touch the wheel of a car again until her birthday. "Such a nuisance!" was the way she dismissed the need to wait until she could procure a valid permit. "You'd think I'd committed a crime or something!"

So far as Midge could judge, she felt not the slightest qualm of shame, only regret over being caught. This attitude was impossible for Midge to understand; still, she couldn't see that it was up to her to try to change it. Basically the matter lay between Sandra and her parents.

But Midge, too, suffered the inconvenience of Sandra's not being permitted to drive. Now when it was time for her to go, Sandra would have to call Pax, or another of her circle of admiring males, and ask him to drive Midge home, an arrangement Midge didn't find exactly flattering.

Later that afternoon Bob Pierson happened to be passing her house on his bike when Pax let her out of his convertible. Bob stood watching glumly as the older boy drove off. "You going out with him now?" he asked.

"Not 'going out,'" Midge said, although she really didn't see what business it was of Bob's. Honesty compelled her to add, "Sandra just had him bring me home."

"He didn't look as if he minded too much," Bob said aggrievedly, "the way you were yacking away when you drove up."

The suspicion that Bob might be a bit jealous amused Midge. "Oh, we get along fine," she said airily.

Bob's scowl deepened. "You know," he accused, "you're beginning to sound smart-alecky and stuck on yourself just like Sandra. I don't know what's the matter with you lately!"

He slid onto his bike and pedaled off angrily into the dusk. Midge smiled faintly, watching him go. Poor old Bob, she thought. When you got right down to it, he was terribly immature.

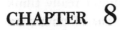

CHAPTER 8

Chance Meeting

Midge found a letter from Tom Brooks awaiting her. Happily she carried it up to her room to read. Their correspondence was irregular, but both of them enjoyed it. This time Tom wrote: "Boy, I miss those talks we used to have! The thing about you is, you've got definite ideas and don't hesitate to state them. Most of the girls around here are unwilling to express an opinion unless they know that whomever they're talking to feels the same way on the subject. A reasonable amount of disagreement is more exciting. That's why we had such a ball last summer. We were always arguing something or other, not just yessing each other's opinions. But then, I guess there aren't too many around like you, kid. You're an original. Just be sure you stay that way. I'm counting on it."

When she had finished Tom's letter, Midge sat staring off thoughtfully into space. Coming so closely on the heels of Bob's accusation that she was beginning to sound like Sandra, it made her wonder whether indeed she had changed. But she didn't really think so. Tom was exaggerating the number of points on which they hadn't seen eye to eye. And she still had definite opinions, nor did she hesitate to voice them, except——. She frowned, realizing that she held her tongue occasionally with Sandra when she knew their viewpoints differed drastically. But Sandra was her friend and Midge valued their friendship. There was no reason to stick one's neck out and make a big issue out of every little area of disagreement. Look at all Sandra had done for her, including her in double dates almost every weekend, opening the way for her into a hitherto closed circle. Why should she risk all that for the privilege of being, as Tom had called her, an original? After all there was such a thing as compromise, and reasonable people didn't frown on it either. If Tom had been at hand, Midge would have told him as much. What was he trying to do, make her feel uncomfortable, as if she weren't being true to herself? He was as bad as Bob!

A few days later, on an afternoon when Sandra was involved in a shopping expedition, Midge stopped by after school to see Miss Tess Wentworth. She felt a small qualm of guilt as she turned up the meticulously swept walk and passed the iron deer on which she used to love to ride as a child. But it had been such a busy fall, she simply hadn't had time to fit in a visit since school started. Miss Tess would understand.

Her repeated ring was finally answered by Miss Tess's elderly housekeeper, who seemed deafer than ever but no less cheerful with her advancing years. She welcomed Midge warmly, then ushered her to the wide doorway opening into the beautifully maintained old-fashioned parlor. Stepping into this room with its lovely, time-softened colors, its rose-patterned carpet, and brocade drapes always seemed to Midge like a step backward in time to a more leisurely and gracious period. And Miss Tess herself, white hair drawn back simply from her bone-sharp but still distinguished features, fitted her surroundings to perfection. She sat on a crimson damask chair, her feet on a low stool, a soft knitted throw across her knees. But her eyes were bright and alive with interest, and her thin hand pressed Midge's warmly as she made her welcome.

"How kind of you to come," Miss Tess said, waving Midge toward a chair opposite her own. "You'll have tea with me, won't you? I was just going to have it brought in."

"I'd love to." Midge relaxed into the tall wing-backed chair with a little sigh, letting the magic of the room seep into her. "I've missed you, but I've been terribly busy."

Miss Tess's nod was understanding. "I'm sure you have. These are such busy days, and you are at an age when you must naturally get involved in a great many activities. There just aren't enough hours in the day or days in the week to hold all the things you want so urgently to do. I can remember how it was long ago, when I was young."

"Was it fun then too?" Midge asked.

"A lovely age," Miss Tess nodded reminiscently.

71

"There is a couplet—I can't recall which poet wrote it—that goes, "Standing with reluctant feet, where the brook and river meet." I always thought that very descriptive."

"Only no one," Midge's smile was wry, "seems reluctant anymore. We sort of rush ahead to meet whatever comes next."

Miss Tess smiled too. "I suppose girls always felt that way deep inside. But your generation is more avid about getting into the thick of things at an early age. I read an article the other day that said going steady has become quite common among children in seventh and eighth grades. Is that true?"

"I'm afraid so," Midge admitted.

A small chuckle escaped Miss Tess. "When I was young," she said, "the very term 'going steady' was an object of derision. The practice was brought to this country by one of the large immigrant groups and the only people who went steady were servant girls and their swains. Young people of any degree of culture and refinement considered it a barbarous custom."

"Maybe they were right," Midge said. "It is pretty barbarous. The trouble is, it limits you so. And if you go steady long enough, you begin to get the stupid idea that you want to marry as soon as you're through high school, or even before, in some cases. I think the whole business is crazy."

The old woman nodded in agreement. "Life should be a glorious adventure at your age, a reaching out. Any practice which tends to dull or narrow it is regrettable."

Talking with Miss Tess, drinking tea and eating little paper-thin sandwiches and delicious cookies from the fragile Haviland china brought from France by Miss Tess's father, Midge felt some of the tension of everyday living slip away. She was relaxed and quietly happy, almost detached. Here in Miss Tess's calm presence, among the ornate furniture and family pictures, it was as if Midge stood apart and studied herself quite impersonally. Why do you get into such a stew, this other self asked curiously? Why do you try to cram so much into every hour, every minute? Of course you must do your schoolwork, but you could easily eliminate some of your other activities. There isn't enough time left over simply to be you, to do the things you really enjoy most of all—the quiet, personal sort of things, such as reading just for the joy of it, going for walks through the woods and horseback rides away out in the country, as Judy and you loved to do. When you get right down to it, haven't you lost your perspective a bit lately? And isn't it about time you slowed down enough to figure out just where you're going and whether, when you get there, you'll find it's where you want to be?

Midge told Miss Tess, "I'm awfully glad I came to see you. It's done me a lot of good."

When the old woman smiled, her pink cheeks crinkled like delicate paper into countless tiny lines. "I'm glad you came, too, my dear. But how have I helped you?"

"I don't know exactly," Midge admitted. "But being here with you—well, it makes wanting to be in on all

73

the school activities and trying so hard to be popular seem such a rat-race sort of thing."

"Girls have always wanted to be popular," Miss Tess said gently. "I don't suppose that will ever change. But it does seem to me, judging by what I read, that the concept of being well liked has become almost a national purpose in America. Not only among young people, either. We want all the world to like us, to approve of us wholeheartedly. But isn't it more important, truly, that, as a nation, we be respected because we are honorable in our dealings with other countries and stand for right values?"

Midge nodded. But she didn't really want to get off on the larger issues facing America. She was too wound up at the moment with the small, but personally vital, issues facing Midge Heydon. She said, "We're always being told we must develop a sense of values and stick to it. And yet no one says much any more about—oh, things like responsibility, duty, ethics, even right or wrong. It's considered hopelessly corny. You're a square at school if you get all shook over cheating in exams. Most of the kids won't cheat themselves, but they're afraid of being considered holier-than-thou if they won't let someone else take a peek at their answers. Still, it's not right and we know it."

"There seem to be many problems these days," Miss Tess said sympathetically. "And your generation will no doubt have to find its own way, just as the generations that came before did. I feel, though, that if one can maintain the courage of one's own convictions, it should be possible to work things out."

74

Midge thought, but did not say aloud, that it was even considered rather corny to have convictions nowadays. The accepted procedure was just to go along with the crowd. But sitting there in Miss Tess's parlor, under the stern gaze of all the long-dead Wentworths in their carved gilt picture frames, this floating along with the current seemed quite shameful. Still, who wanted to risk being considered a square?

It was almost dusk when Midge said good-by to Miss Tess and started toward home. She was glad she had several blocks to walk. Maybe there would be time to sort out the rather confused feelings and uncertainties that her talk with the old woman seemed to have stirred up, rather than settled.

She passed a tall boy in a Loden coat who was walking in the same direction she was, but at a slower pace. Then, belatedly realizing it was someone she knew, she glanced back with a little apologetic, "Hi, Hans. I didn't recognize you."

"Hi, Midge." He caught up with her in two long strides. "I wasn't quite sure who you were, either. Where are you rushing so fast?"

"Was I rushing?" Midge smiled, as they walked on together. "I'm just going home."

"Americans always rush," Hans grinned, his blue eyes teasing. "You seem to feel that your destination isn't so important as the fact that you are getting there so quickly. In cars or afoot it is the same. I sometimes wonder whether all the time saved by beating another driver away from a stop light or across the next intersection is put to good use."

They laughed together and Midge said ruefully, "I rather doubt it, don't you? Probably when they get where they're going, they don't know what to do with themselves."

"Tell me," Hans asked, "how you happen to be in my neighborhood. I've never seen you on this street before."

"I was visiting an old friend," Midge told him. "I mean that both ways. Miss Tess is very old and we've been friends since I was a little girl. She lives in that big gingerbready house back at the corner."

It seemed the most natural thing in the world to tell Hans all about Miss Tess as they strolled along through the blue dusk. He appeared interested, asking questions and making comments. Midge found herself talking to him easily, without self-consciousness. None of the feeling of strain, of trying very hard to be vivacious and appealing, which sometimes drove her when she was out on dates Sandra had arranged for her troubled her now. She could talk as casually with Hans as with Bob, she realized. And yet, talking with Hans, walking along beside him, was different, more warmly exciting than if Bob had been her companion. Midge tried to pin down the elusive difference. When she realized what it was, she felt her mouth twist into a smile. The thing was, Hans didn't seem a bit like a brother, while Bob did.

She was amazed to glance up and see her own familiar house just a few steps ahead. They had walked almost six blocks and it hadn't seemed any distance at all.

"You've come a lot out of your way," Midge exclaimed apologetically. "There was no need for you to do that."

"There was a need," Hans said gravely. "A very great need. Would you like to know what it was?" Then, at Midge's nod, he said, lowering his voice conspiratorially, "I wanted to."

Midge felt herself flushing with pleasure and was grateful for the dusk that hid her heightened color. "I enjoyed it too," she admitted.

"And may I walk with you again?" Hans asked. "Perhaps to a motion picture, or to the drugstore for a hot chocolate, or just to your home some afternoon from school?"

Midge nodded. "I'd like that, Hans."

He pressed her hand in an oddly formal gesture. "Then we shall do it. And very soon. Good evening, Midge."

He turned on his heel and strolled off. Before Midge had crossed the porch and opened her door, she heard a scrap of tune, whistled in a sprightly manner. Was it Hans, she wondered?

A curious sense of pleasure filled her. She felt a little like whistling herself. And all the doubts and questions that had nagged at her when she had left Miss Tess seemed to have been miraculously dissipated. Where had they gone? Midge had no idea. Certainly she hadn't consciously solved them. Yet they no longer weighed heavily on her heart, her spirit. Just being with Hans seemed to have afforded a temporary solution of her problems.

Now only one question loomed large in Midge's mind. Would he seek her out, ask her for a date, as his parting words had seemed to promise? The strength of her hope that she'd see more of Hans Dietrich amazed her.

CHAPTER 9

A Date with Hans

As time passed, Midge grew disturbed over a change that developed in the method of Sandra and her doing their homework together. What had begun as a joint effort gradually reached a stage where Midge seemed to be doing all the work, a shift she resented and didn't feel was entirely honest.

When she said as much, though, Sandra found her complaint merely amusing. "So what if you are better at the grubby details then I? Is that so terrible?"

"But you won't learn much," Midge pointed out. "Or don't you care about that?"

Sandra shook her head. "Not so long as I get by. And, after all," she reminded, "I've done you some favors too."

"Getting me dates, you mean?" Midge said starkly.

"Don't be like that," Sandra's tone was softly appealing. "I love doubling with you. You know that. It makes my date more fun too."

"I don't think the boys you go out with would agree," Midge said dryly. "They'd probably rather dispense with another couple."

Sandra smiled. "It's what I want that matters. If there's one I care to be alone with all evening, we won't double."

"Anyway," Midge went on, "I have a hunch that the boys you get to date me are only doing it so they can be with you too."

"Now why would you think a thing like that?"

"Because they never ask me for a second date on their own." It hurt to admit it, but it was quite true.

"We'll find one you really click with eventually," Sandra soothed. "I honestly think it's your attitude that discourages them. You are pretty stand-offish and cool."

"I'm not!" Midge denied. "I chatter away till I can't think of a single other thing to say. I do everything I can to make them like me and think I'm fun."

"Couldn't you defrost and be a little more inviting?"

"Oh, honestly!" Midge said.

"I'm only being realistic." Sandra shrugged.

Midge said slowly, "I happened to run into Hans Dietrich the other day. He walked me home and didn't seem to find me a bit forbidding. In fact he practically asked me for a date."

"Hans Dietrich?" Sandra laughed. "You can't be serious."

"Why can't I?" Midge demanded. "He's really very nice."

"That may be," Sandra spoke in a sweetly reasonable tone. "But what's the percentage in wasting time on an exchange student who won't even be around next year? Have you thought of that? Besides, where could he take you? He doesn't have a car."

"I don't care!" Midge said much more heatedly than she usually spoke to Sandra. "You're always figuring angles! He's nice and I like him. And if he asks me for a date, I'll go!"

Sandra's speculative, dark gaze rested on Midge for a long moment. Then she said mildly, "Don't get all shook up over it. You can certainly date anyone you please. It's just—well, when you've begun to be accepted by the crowd that really matters at school, isn't it a little childish to throw it all away for a boy you scarcely know, who simply isn't anybody?"

"But he *is* somebody," Midge argued, surprised at the depth of her resentment. "He's——"

"You know what I mean," Sandra interrupted. "But let's not get into a hassle over him. He's not that important. Maybe he won't even ask you to go out. And speaking of going out," she changed the subject adroitly, "I've decided to stop doing just that with Rick."

"You have?" Midge was taken by surprise. "But I thought you liked him a lot."

"I did," Sandra said lightly. "But nothing lasts forever. And Rick's beginning to think he owns me, so I figure the time has come to let him know he's wrong."

Midge didn't say anything for a moment. She felt a rush of envy for Sandra. How could she be so con-

One of the Crowd

fident, so sure of her own attraction that she could afford to toss a big-man-around-school like Rick Lewis aside so casually? And if she, Midge, spent enough time with her, was it possible she might acquire some of Sandra's assurance, might become sufficiently attractive and sure of herself to pick and choose which boy she would favor with her company? It didn't seem likely, but a girl could hope.

She asked wonderingly, "You didn't have a fight or anything? You're just going to call it quits?"

Sandra shook her head. "No fights. And I've already called it quits. I've made it a point to avoid Rick all week at school. If he hasn't got the message yet, he's pretty stupid."

"But if he does ask you for a date this weekend, what will you say?"

"That I'm all dated up with Ben Blanchard."

"Poor Rick," Midge murmured. Ben was a darkly handsome junior who had played leads in several school plays. He had a red convertible and an apparently inexhaustible allowance.

"Don't waste your sympathy," Sandra shrugged. "Maybe Rick will learn he can't take too much for granted. Besides, he's beginning to bore me."

"Probably Ben will, too, after a while. You seem to have a pretty low boring point."

"That's very clever," Sandra said with a chuckle. "I must remember it. And I suppose it's true, actually." She told Midge then, "After Ben and I have a few dates, enough to get better acquainted, I'll have him get someone for you and we'll double."

82

"You needn't do that." Midge knew it was unreasonable for her to feel a small prod of resentment. But Sandra sounded smug, almost condescending. Or was she just imagining that, Midge wondered, because of her own sense of inadequacy?

Sandra's tone was warm, assuring Midge, "I know I needn't. I just happen to want to. Aren't we friends?"

Midge felt her questioning uncertainty fade under the charm of Sandra's smile, the sincerity of her wide, candid glance. "Of course," she said gratefully. How could she have forgotten, even for a moment, how lucky she was to have Sandra for a friend?

One Friday in Chemistry Midge found herself cleaning up after a lab experiment along with Hans and a couple of other students. When they had finished and she and Hans were hanging their aprons away, he said a trifle hesitantly, "If you have not already made other plans for this evening, I wonder whether you would care to go to the motion—I mean the movies," he corrected himself with a smile. "There is an English comedy which has been well spoken of——"

Before his voice could run down entirely, Midge nodded and said with pleasure, "I'd love to, Hans. When shall I be ready?"

"Eight o'clock? We'll have to walk, you know," his tone was apologetic.

"That's okay," Midge said. "It's only a few blocks. We'll easily be in time for the second show."

She dressed for her date that night with unusual

83

care. Casual clothes, of course, for a mere movie; still, Midge was glad her blue bulky-knit sweater was newly laundered, and thankful her hair fell softly and naturally the way she wanted it. Both her parents were eager to meet Hans and, when he arrived, Midge took him into the living room, where a fire crackled brightly on the hearth and the muted music of Beethoven on the record player afforded a background to their few moments' talk. Rather oddly Hans seemed more sure of himself and at ease in conversation with her parents than he did with younger people. And she could tell that both of them were favorably impressed with him.

Later, as they walked through the chill, starlit night toward the theater, Hans said, "They are so friendly, your parents, so warm and with—" he searched for the right word, "heart."

Midge smiled. "Yes, they are like that."

"You, too," Hans said shyly. "I felt this warmth, this friendliness in you from the start. Even that first night at the Mixer when I was so clumsy."

"You weren't clumsy," Midge objected. "It was the other boy's fault."

"No matter," Hans said with a little chuckle. "It was I who got spilled upon. Probably now that I have been here longer it wouldn't bother me so much. But then, even though I wanted so very much to stay and spend more time with you, get better acquainted— well, I could think of nothing else to do but leave."

Midge felt a quiver of pleasure stir her at his words. She said, her tone teasing, "Why did you wait so long to try again?"

A Date with Hans

"You are so popular," Hans said frankly, "always with such a gay crowd, having so much fun, laughing and making jokes among yourselves. I thought I might be intruding myself on you. But then that day when we happened to meet as you walked home from the house of your elderly friend—well, you seemed in such a pensive, quiet mood, and as if you did not find me too dull."

"You're not dull," Midge said seriously. "In fact, you're very interesting. And just because I'm with other kids at school, that doesn't mean you wouldn't be welcome to join us too."

Hans smiled down at her, a rather wry smile. "Maybe you would welcome me, but I'm not sure the others would feel the same. Many students here are kind and helpful and friendly. Others, some of your friends among them, I fear, have some such idea as, 'Oh, he's strange and different—an outsider. Why should we bother with him when we are so important?' You see what I mean?"

"Well, I don't feel that way," Midge told him.

"Good!" Hans's gloved hand pressed her elbow briefly. "I am glad of that." He went on then in a philosophical sort of tone, "Please don't think I'm trying to say it might not be the same in my country where someone from a foreign land is concerned. Intolerance is not the failing of any one nationality. There are such people in many parts of the world. One ignores their dislike, brushes it aside like a cobweb and goes on to find the others who are different. There are so many more who are kind and friendly."

As Midge and he walked along, they talked easily, effortlessly on any number of topics. Hans told her of his trip to the United States by plane under the auspices of an international youth-exchange program; he mentioned his parents and two sisters back in Bavaria. But when Midge asked if that was his birthplace, his face and tone sobered as he told how the family had had to escape by night from their former home when the Communists occupied that territory. "I was just a child then," Hans said, "but I can remember hiding in barns during the daytime and hurrying, hurrying by night, with a black sense of fear driving us all. My mother wept for the family possessions she had to leave behind. But we were fortunate. My father's training as an engineer made it possible for him to establish another home for us. And it is all far in the past now and better forgotten. I think, though, that the basis for my strong urge to study in America lay in that experience. I feel it is such a vital thing for the young people of different countries to understand each other, to grasp each other's way of life, the beliefs and traditions. Then maybe the insanity of war cannot be and peace will have a chance——" he broke off apologetically. "I'm sorry. I forget that here it is what you call 'square' to talk so seriously."

"It's not," Midge denied. "I feel as you do, that exchange programs, young people getting to know each other, are our best hope for the future."

Both of them glanced up in surprise as the garish

lights of the movie marquee fell on their faces. "How did we get here so fast?" Midge asked wonderingly.

And Hans shook his bare blond head, admitting, "I don't know. Usually that walk is much longer."

The comedy was delightful. Sitting in the dark theater, their shoulders touching companionably, Midge and Hans laughed uproariously and ate popcorn and forgot all about serious matters. Afterward they stopped at Joe's Grill down the block for hot chocolate. The place was well filled with their contemporaries and noisy with talk and laughter and jukebox music.

"But I like Beethoven better," Hans confided to Midge.

"So do I," Midge smiled conspiratorially. "Only this sort of thing's much better for dancing."

"Ah yes," Hans nodded. "But there in your living room it was like meeting an old friend. He made me feel at home, welcome."

"We have lots of classical records," Midge said. "Why don't you come over and listen to your favorites some evening?"

"This would not bore you?" Hans asked.

"Of course not," Midge said. "I often play them myself. And Mom and Dad love them."

"Then I will take you up on this kind offer," Hans beamed. "When may I come? Tomorrow?"

Midge's heart quickened as she answered, "Tomorrow will be fine."

CHAPTER 10

The Rally

Bob Pierson stopped by one evening to ask Midge to go with him to an antique-car rally to be held in Beechville, a town some twenty miles from Edgewood.

"What fun!" she exclaimed, her eyes sparkling. "But how can you drive when you haven't a license yet?"

"Don't worry," Bob told her. "That's all arranged."

"You mean you've actually found someone else you'll trust with that car?"

Bob scowled. "Very funny! If you hadn't been so busy lately, you'd know I have. Terry Blaine and I have taken her out on trial runs several times. He handles her just right."

"Terry Blaine?" Midge repeated, reminded fleetingly of Sandra, who had once gone steady with Terry, but had nothing to do with him now. "I didn't even know you knew him."

"Sure," Bob nodded, "he's in my Physics class. And

ever since I found out he's as crazy about vintage cars as I am, I've been letting him drive the Duchess."

"So you finally named her," Midge smiled. "Very appropriate." She asked then, struck by a sudden thought, "But if he's going with you, how come I'm included?"

"He's asking a girl too," Bob explained. Then, after a moment, he went on a trifle uncomfortably, "I was wondering whether your friend, Miss Wentworth, has any old clothes—oh, from away back around the time the Duchess was new, or even earlier."

"Now I get it," Midge teased. "That's why I'm invited."

"Don't be like that," Bob growled. "I'd like to have you go along anyway. But lots of people do dress up at rallies. So if you wouldn't mind helping us find some old costumes . . ."

Miss Tess's attic proved richly equal to the occasion. And Miss Tess herself evinced a lively interest in the entire undertaking. From her chair, strategically placed at the foot of the steep attic stairs, she directed Midge's and Bob's search like a general behind the lines sending troops into action. Dusters and motoring caps which had belonged to her father were found for the boys. And Midge selected two coats, one emerald-green and the other a bright blue, both with high shawl collars and large white buttons, for herself and whomever Terry invited to go along. With these, Miss Tess told Midge, they should wear large hats, tied on with transparent scarves or veils. "There's a whole trunkful of hats and veils up there," she called generously. "Pick out any you want."

"This is so wonderful of you," Midge told her later, while the housekeeper was packing the clothes into boxes for Midge and Bob to take home. "We surely appreciate it."

"You're very welcome," Miss Tess beamed.

Bob told her, "If you'd like to see how we look, we can drive past Saturday as we start out. I'd like to have you see the way I've fixed the car up too."

"That would be such a treat," Miss Tess said warmly. "I'll be watching for you."

Walking home with their loot, Midge queried, "Isn't she a darling? I'm glad you offered to drive past."

"Seemed like the least I could do," Bob grinned. "After all, I wouldn't have the Duchess if it weren't for her."

"And for me!" Midge couldn't resist reminding him. She thought to ask then, "Do you know whom Terry's taking?"

Bob nodded. "Tricia Farnham. You know her, don't you?"

Midge frowned slightly. "Yes, but I didn't realize she and Terry still went together. Didn't they break up once?"

"How should I know?" Bob's tone indicated a vast disinterest in all such details. "All he told me was that he'd asked Tricia and she was going. Why? Don't you like her, or what?"

"I don't know her very well," Midge said guardedly.

After all, it wasn't fair to condemn someone on the basis of things you'd heard, even though you'd heard them from as good a friend as Sandra. She went on, "In a way, I'm glad she's going. Spending the whole afternoon with her, I should be able to find out what she's like for myself."

"You make it all sound like a big fat mystery," Bob said disgustedly. "Have you heard some stupid gossip, or something? Girls are good at that, always tearing each other apart."

"We don't gossip any more than boys do," Midge argued.

And they were off in a lively discussion of the faults and merits of the sexes that lasted all the way home.

When Sandra heard Midge's plans for Saturday, she shook her head wonderingly. "An old-car rally? How corny can you get! I can imagine Bob doing that sort of thing, but not you."

"I think it'll be fun," Midge said, her tone defensive. "There'll be a tour of all the cars through certain streets in Beechville. Then awards will be given for the oldest car and the best job of restoration and the most authentic costumes and so on. And then this association of antique-car owners is giving a dinner party at the hotel. What's so corny about that?"

"If you don't know, I couldn't explain it."

It seemed to Midge, as hot resentment rose in her at her friend's attitude, that Sandra considered everything corny except half a dozen favored activities of the crowd. To read a book for pleasure, to like to walk, to enjoy listening to classical records, to play bridge with your parents—the list of interests and activities that Sandra condemned grew long in Midge's mind. Dates, not only in Sandra's opinion but in that of other members of the crowd as well, must follow certain well-defined lines. Friday nights you went to the movies. Or you might bowl with a group of your intimates, or go to some school-centered activity such as a class play or sports event or a dance. Some school clubs carried a considerable measure of prestige, and these were favored by the crowd. Others were considered strictly for peasants and carefully avoided. Saturday nights were for big dates, dinner and dancing, perhaps the theater if any road companies were playing within driving distance of Edgewood. Or people sometimes had parties, the informal, carefully unplanned type. Midge had not, as yet, been invited to any of these, since she was so newly one of the crowd. But she had heard from Sandra that they were lots of fun. You played records and danced in somebody's rec room, with the lights turned very low. There was plenty of food and soft drinks and little or no supervision from parents, who were often having a very gay party of their own in another area of the house. According to Sandra a good deal of necking went on, but it was all quite harmless. "Good clean fun," was the way she put it. Hearing her made little shivers of excitement run down Midge's spine. Because one of these days she would be invited. If not before, at least to the very next party Sandra gave. Sandra had promised as much.

Now, as hot words crowded to her lips, Midge held

92

them back with difficulty. Sandra's attitude was so annoyingly superior. Still, it would be foolish to risk their friendship and all the advantages that Sandra's approval carried with it in order to take a big stand about something as basically unimportant as a date with Bob. For all she knew, Midge reminded herself, the antique-car rally might prove dull and boring. But she wouldn't turn down a chance to attend it because of the mere possibility. She was going to find out for herself.

"Why are you looking at me so oddly?" Sandra asked.

"I was thinking," Midge admitted.

"Not that!" Sandra exclaimed in mock horror. "It only gets you into trouble. Anyway," she went on, "I'm sorry about Saturday for another reason. I was going to suggest that Ben get someone for you so we could double."

"Why didn't you mention it sooner?" Midge felt a small ache of disappointment. "I thought you wanted Ben all to yourself for a while."

"We're pretty well acquainted now," Sandra drawled. "We can stand company. But so long as you're busy we'll get someone else. Maybe Sharon and Kent."

"Another time," Midge told her, "I'd love to." She tried, but wasn't quite able, to dismiss a wholly unworthy suspicion that Sandra had made up all this so she'd feel worse about having promised to go to the rally. But surely a friend wouldn't do such a thing.

"Sure," Sandra nodded. "It's just that I hate to see

you wasting your time on outsiders, when there are so many more attractive boys right in the crowd." The warmth of her smile melted Midge's last lingering doubt and made her feel ashamed of herself for having harbored it.

Saturday was a lovely mild day with a pale wash of sunshine augmenting the colors of autumn. After the promised preliminary stop at Miss Tess's house for her inspection and warm approval, the Duchess and her four costumed passengers sped smartly off down the highway toward Beechville. Their rate of speed was modest, but it felt as though they were going much faster, due to the fact that the car was a touring model with open sides through which the wind whistled. Midge and Tricia, laughing and rosy in the breeze, hung onto their big hats for dear life.

"Now I know why they tied them on with scarves," Midge said wryly.

"And even that doesn't help much," Tricia answered, brushing a strand of hair from her eyes.

Just at first, Midge had felt a little stiff and strange with both Tricia and Terry, having heard so much about them in advance. But the casual friendliness of their manner, the easy naturalness of their personalities, soon dissipated her mood. Why, they were as nice as could be, she told herself with some surprise. Or at least they seemed so. Maybe Sandra was mistaken in her opinion of them. Or they could have changed. At any rate, Midge decided, she was going to accept them at face value until something they did or said proved that her agreeable reaction to them was mistaken. And certainly, during a whole afternoon and evening spent together, she should be able to form a valid opinion of her own.

The trip to Beechville was quite an experience. Other cars slowed down so that their occupants could have a better look at this unusual vehicle, and everyone smiled and waved. The four in the Duchess waved back in equally friendly fashion. When they arrived at their destination, Bob registered his car and then they joined in the colorful procession which assembled near the town square and proceeded to drive sedately about the streets, where crowds of onlookers had gathered. Later there was the serious judging of the antique cars and the authenticity of their owners' costumes, the results of which would be announced at dinner.

A wonderful spirit of camaraderie seemed to exist among vintage-car enthusiasts, Midge discovered. They were a breed apart and, although most of them were older than the four from Edgewood, this didn't seem to make the slightest difference. The men gathered in little knots, discussing motors and rates of speed and the challenging difficulty of securing needed parts and equipment. Many of the women drifted into the lobby of the hotel to get warm after their air-conditioned rides, and Midge and Tricia found themselves a part of a pleasant, friendly group that made them feel quite at ease. One of the oldest couples, they learned, were driving the 1929 Packard in which they had made their wedding trip. Another pair were progressing enthusiastically backward, having first owned a 1931 Bentley, then a 1912 Oakland, and were now dickering to purchase a really priceless treasure, a 1909 Simplex.

"It's sort of like an epidemic," Tricia confided to Midge. "Do you suppose we're immune or will we be infected?"

"Right now my resistance is pretty low," Midge smiled. "It sounds like a lot of fun. But maybe when I get out of this atmosphere, I'll recover."

"Terry's mad about the Duchess," Tricia said, her tone warming as she spoke of him. "He'd give a lot to find a car that compares with her. But usually one that old is quite expensive."

"I know," Midge nodded. "Bob got a break."

"You got it for him, I understand," Tricia said. "And he's everlastingly grateful, too." She sighed. "Unfortunately I don't know anyone who has an antique auto lying around loose, so I can't be a fairy godmother for Terry."

Long before the evening was over, Midge had begun to feel very well acquainted with Tricia. They had talked a lot and the forthright openness of the other girl's nature made it hard to believe that she was pretending to be something she wasn't. But how could Sandra have been so mistaken about her, Midge wondered? Or was Tricia more devious than she seemed on the surface? One thing Midge felt sure of: Tricia's and Terry's fondness for each other was real and deep. There was no doubt of the strong attraction between them. It shone clearly and warmly, like a flame.

After dinner in the big, chandelier-lit private dining

room of the hotel, the awards were given. And Midge felt her heart swell with pride and pleasure as Bob went happily forward to receive the medal for "best-preserved car." There were older cars and some of the owners had worn more striking costumes, but the Duchess had come through handsomely even in such distinguished company. All those hours Bob had lavished on her motor and brasswork and upholstery had proved worth while.

Afterward there was dancing, but Tricia and Midge and the boys stayed for only a few numbers. It was a fairly long drive home, and motors as old as that of the Duchess had been known to give trouble. But the distance back to Edgewood was covered without mishap. The moon was silver-bright and there were millions of stars. Midge and the others sang all the way home, songs old and new, lively and sentimental. A mood of happy well-being wrapped them about. It had been a wonderful day from start to finish.

Thanking Bob, saying good night as she was let out in front of her house, Midge said, "It was such fun! I can't remember when I've had a better time."

And as the others agreed wholeheartedly, Midge heard Tricia saying in the friendliest way, "We'll have to get together again soon."

"Yes," Midge answered, "I'd like that."

And, rather to her own surprise, she found that she meant it.

CHAPTER 11

A Talk with Tobey

With the approach of Thanksgiving, all thoughts in the Heydon household were directed toward the imminent return home of Tobey and Brose for the long weekend holiday. Midge was especially delighted at the prospect of seeing her favorite sister. Tobey, although seven years older than she, had always been sympathetic toward her problems and uncertainties, and Midge valued her opinion highly and had always found her advice most helpful. Now, not having seen Tobey for months, she had accumulated a large number of things that needed talking over.

Tobey and Brose, looking a bit tired after their eight-hour train trip, but obviously happy, arrived so late on Thanksgiving Eve that there was little chance for conversation that night. The holiday itself was filled with the preparation of dinner and the subsequent serving and eating of the lavish meal. Midge had no opportunity to get Tobey alone for even a minute. All day

long and well into the evening the house swarmed
with people. Alicia and Adam and the baby were
there, as were Adam's father, the widowed Mr. Wentworth, and his aunt Miss Tess, fragile as an ancient
Dresden china figurine in her elegant old-fashioned
silks and laces. The Heydons would have included
Brose's parents, too, in the big family party, if it hadn't
been that they were out of town, visiting his grand-
parents.

The house echoed with talk and laughter. Cannel
coal crackled in the fireplace, there were flowers about,
and the pleasant aroma of good food filled the air.
This was what Thanksgiving had always been, as far
back as Midge could remember. So it would always be.
A sense of warmth, of security was distilled in her here
with the people she loved, under the roof that had
always meant home to her. She was happy without
bothering to analyze her feelings or give the matter
the slightest thought.

Late in the afternoon, soon after she had finished
helping with the dishes, Midge heard the phone ring
and went out into the hall to answer it. Sandra's
voice reached her.

"Midge, you busy?" she asked in a bored tone.

"Not too busy to talk," Midge told her. "Why?"

They were on as friendly terms as ever, even friend-
lier in some ways. Midge had been afraid Sandra
might resent her having been with Tricia Farnham at
the rally. And Sandra's first reaction had been one of
veiled anger. She had demanded to know whether
Tricia had said anything about her. But when Midge

denied this, Sandra's attitude had altered and she had agreed that, of course, Midge had a perfect right to spend her time with anyone she chose. However, aside from casually friendly encounters at school and at club meetings, Midge found she saw scarcely any more of Tricia than before. This was due to the fact that Sandra had included her in dates almost every weekend, and with boys so popular that Midge felt flattered to be seen with them. She had managed to save some time for Hans. But there had been no opportunity at all to double date with Bob and Tricia and Terry. This Midge honestly regretted. But whenever Bob had suggested it, she'd already had something else planned.

Now Sandra asked, "How about coming over for a while?"

"You mean now? Oh, I couldn't," Midge told her. It seemed more polite to put it that way than to say frankly she didn't want to. "There's a mob here. We're having a family party."

"Yes, but can't *you* get away? If there's such a mob, they'll never miss you." She went on before Midge could answer, "I'm home alone. My parents have gone to a cocktail party. I'll call Ben and he can get someone for you and we'll——"

"Sandra, I can't," Midge broke in, feeling pity stir in her sharply. "I wouldn't dream of going anywhere tonight. But why don't you come over here? We'd love to have you."

"No, thanks," Sandra said with an airy little laugh. "I can't stand family parties. If you can't make it, I'll try Debbie."

100

A *Talk with Tobey*

"But I want you to meet my sister Tobey while she's here," Midge reminded. "This would be such a good chance."

"Maybe tomorrow," Sandra said indefinitely, "when there aren't so many people around."

"But you're sure you can get someone tonight——" Midge began, troubled by the thought of Sandra alone, or with only the grumpy housekeeper and her silent husband for company.

"Don't worry," Sandra broke in. "I know I can count on Ben at least. 'Bye now. See you."

At the click of the receiver dropping into place, Midge hung up, too, and went slowly back to join the others.

The following morning afforded the chance for the long talk with Tobey she'd been wanting. Dad was at work, Brose had gone off to look up some of his old cronies, and Mom was busy in the kitchen. When Tobey went upstairs to straighten her bedroom soon after breakfast, Midge trailed along with an offer to help.

As they worked, they talked. And when they had put the room to rights, Midge curled up on the bed and Tobey sat in the slipper chair and their conversation continued. Midge told her sister all about her friendship with Sandra and the rewards and complications it entailed. "I want you to meet her," Midge said earnestly. "She'll probably drop in sometime today."

"I hope she does," Tobey said. "I'd like to meet her.

She sounds quite interesting. What does Mom think of her?"

"I don't believe she likes her too well," Midge admitted unhappily. "But that's because Mom doesn't really understand her. She hasn't had the chance to get to know her very well."

"And that's because you go to Sandra's house so much more often than she comes here," Tobey said thoughtfully.

Midge nodded. "It's such a wonderful place to study. We have it practically all to ourselves—and it's so gorgeous!"

"You seem to like Sandra a lot," Tobey went on, "and yet you say she's not nearly as congenial as Judy was, that her ideas are quite different from yours. Are you sure," she asked with an understanding little smile, "that it's really Sandra you like, or just the prestige that being friends with her involves?"

Instead of answering, Midge asked another question. "Would it be so terrible if that did enter into it? Being her friend has put me into one of the smoothest crowds at school. And she's got me dates with some wonderful boys——"

"Boys you really like?" Tobey broke in.

Midge stared at her. "Well—I can't say I've been mad about any of them, but they're all real wheels at school and lots of the other girls are green with envy. In fact sometimes I can hardly believe it's happening myself."

Tobey's smile was gentle. "And yet I get the idea that the dates you enjoy most are those you've had

102

with that German boy, Hans, that Sandra tried to talk you out of bothering with. You even had more fun with Bob when he took you to something interesting and different like that old-car rally."

"Only because Tricia and Terry were along too," Midge said firmly. "Ordinarily—well, Bob seems more like a brother. As for Hans—" she hesitated a moment, wanting to be entirely honest, "I can't deny that I do find him attractive and awfully interesting. But actually, except for a couple of movies, our dates haven't been real dates at all. He just drops over to talk, or listen to records, or sometimes we go for walks. That sort of thing isn't really considered dating."

"By whom?" Tobey asked.

"By the crowd," Midge explained. "They fig-ure——"

"Isn't it how you figure that's more important? Surely you, little old independent Midge," Tobey smiled, "haven't begun to let outsiders do your think-ing for you." At Midge's startled look she went on, "You certainly don't have to listen to my advice, honey, but you did ask for it. Maybe I'm not qualified to give any, because I'll admit frankly that I never got into one of the terribly smooth crowds at school. I had lots of fun, though, so it never really bothered me. In fact it seemed to me there was something pretty snobbish about forming a tight little clique and as-sociating only with each other. You shut yourself off from so many interesting people that way; you miss out on so much. I guess it's just a matter of deciding what's most important to you and then going after that. If it's friendship with Sandra and being included in her crowd—well, you've got that. But if you're beginning to feel limited and hedged in, I suppose you'll just have to let Sandra know that's how you feel about it."

"She might drop me entirely then," Midge said bleakly.

"I suppose so," Tobey nodded. "But there are lots of other girls at school—you said you liked Tricia——"

"Yes, but Sandra says she's not to be trusted."

"Don't you think it's best to find out about people for yourself," Tobey asked, "not just accept second-hand opinions?"

"Yes, but Sandra knows her lots better than I do," Midge sighed. "And I don't really want to quarrel with Sandra. I like her too well. I'll bet you will, too, when you meet her. . . ."

Rather than clarifying her dilemma, their talk left Midge feeling more mixed up than ever. She had meant to tell Tobey even more, to confide her growing resentment over the amount of homework she was doing for Sandra, perhaps to confess having written the English theme for her. The guilty knowledge of that still formed a dark core deep within her. But somehow she couldn't pour it all out to Tobey, lest her sister be influenced even more strongly against her friend.

Midge was delighted when Sandra dropped in later that day. Brose was back by then and he and Tobey and Sandra and Mom and Midge sat in the firelit living room, talking and eating cookies and drinking hot

A *Talk with Tobey*

chocolate. The conversation was casual and agreeable. Sandra was polite, almost formal, as she always seemed to be with older people. She laughed, but with restraint at Brose's story of all the mishaps that had befallen Tobey the time she tried to entertain two of his senior professors and their wives at dinner. The refrigerator had gone haywire, freezing everything solid. The young couple in the adjoining apartment had had to rush their baby to the hospital when he was threatened with pneumonia, and Tobey had been too sympathetic to decline to keep their active three-year-old while they were gone.

"Dinner was a mess," Tobey recalled with a wry smile, "after all my careful planning and the hours I'd spent on that fancy dessert. The roast was tough and little Nancy upset her milk twice, but everyone was most understanding. In fact, we actually had more fun and got better acquainted than we probably could have if it had all gone as smoothly as I'd intended."

"And how about the baby?" Mom asked. "Is he all right?"

"Oh, he's fine," Brose assured her. "And my wife made such a hit with the faculty brass that night that I've been getting preferential treatment ever since."

"Oh, stop it," Tobey said. "They've just begun to realize what a good job you're doing." The glance she sent him was filled with quiet pride and warmed with love.

"Why do you want to teach?" Sandra asked curiously. "Doesn't private industry offer more pay and opportunity?"

"It undoubtedly offers more pay," Brose answered, "but opportunity? I guess that depends on how you define the word. If by opportunity you mean a chance to do something worthwhile and lasting, then teaching is an excellent field. And, of course, when I finish graduate work and can get a full professorship, the pay will improve, too. Not," he added dryly, "that we're ever likely to be rich."

Sandra smiled politely and did not pursue the subject.

The talk drifted pleasantly to other topics; still, Midge couldn't rid herself of a troubled hunch that Sandra wasn't making too good an impression on Tobey. Nor, for that matter, was Sandra as drawn to Tobey as Midge had wistfully hoped might be the case. A barrier seemed to separate them, composed of differing ideas, varying viewpoints. The same basic lack of understanding with which Mom viewed Sandra seemed to Midge to be forming in Tobey too.

Later that evening, during a brief moment when the two sisters happened to be alone, Midge asked flatly, "You didn't like Sandra very well, did you?"

"Why do you think that?" Tobey's brows lifted. "She was quite charming. Oh, there's a difference in the way we look at lots of things, but I certainly don't dislike her."

"Now you sound like Mom," Midge accused. There was an ache in her throat that made her voice quite husky. "Ever so many people think as Sandra does, that you have to make money in order to be success-

106

ful. People like us, who look at it differently—well, we're in the minority."

"I know we are," Tobey nodded, smiling faintly, "but that doesn't mean we're wrong."

"It's not fair, though," Midge said hotly, "to hold it against Sandra just because——"

"Midge," Tobey's voice broke in quietly, "I'm not holding anything against her. She has a right to her opinion, just as we have a right to ours. And I'm not trying to stop you from being friends with her. If I thought you could influence her, I'd be all in favor of it." She paused for a moment, then went on, her tone light, but with an underlying note of earnestness, "It's only if it works out the other way around that I'll regret it. You see, I happen to be pretty fond of you just the way you are."

CHAPTER **12**

The Least a Friend Can Do

There was another person Midge was eager to have Tobey meet while she was home, and he stopped by Saturday afternoon to return a book he had borrowed. Tobey seemed drawn to Hans at once, and Brose and he proved quite congenial. When Brose heard that Hans, too, was planning on a teaching career, he was able to offer some advice and suggestions for which the German boy was most grateful.

When it was time for Hans to go, he and Midge stood talking for a few minutes in the hall. His tone was a shade wistful as he asked, "I suppose you will be busy tonight with your family?"

"Not especially," Midge told him. "Tobey and Brose are going out with some old friends from their high school days."

"The Armstrongs aren't using their tickets for the

concert series, so they gave them to me," Hans explained. "Would you care to go with me to hear a symphony orchestra?"

"I'd love to," Midge said, her heart giving a small skip of pleasure. "What time shall I be ready?"

"Eight o'clock?" Hans suggested, smiling. "That will give us plenty of time. I'm so glad you're free."

"So am I," Midge admitted.

A warm glow enveloped her as she went back to the living room to join the others. Tobey and Brose were sitting very close together on the couch and Tobey had the happy, satisfied look of a girl who has just been thoroughly kissed.

"Okay, so we've been smooching," Brose admitted with a grin. "Want to make something of it?"

"You mean that goes on even after you're married?" Midge teased. "I had no idea!"

"You'll learn," Tobey told her contentedly. She added then, "I like Hans. He's as nice as you led me to believe and that's saying a good deal."

"Seems intelligent, too," Brose nodded. "I can't imagine what he sees in Midge, though. Can you, Tobey?"

"Okay," Midge made a face at him. "That indicates that he's not only intelligent, but also has superior taste. And you know what? He's taking me to a concert tonight."

"How nice!" Tobey exclaimed.

The phone rang and Midge hurried out to the hall to answer it. Sandra's voice reached her. "I hope you're not still all involved with family?"

"Why, no, not too much," Midge began, "but——"

"Good," Sandra broke in cheerfully. "The crowd's getting together tonight and driving over to that new dine-and-dance place near Beechville. Want to come along?"

"Gee, Sandra, I can't," Midge said, disappointment swelling in her. Why did things always have to come in twos?

"You mean your folks won't let you?" Sandra queried.

"Well, they're not very keen on that sort of thing," Midge had to admit. "But I don't know whether they'd object or not. The thing is, I already have a date for tonight—with Hans."

"Oh, no!" Sandra said disgustedly. "What's he doing, taking you for a walk, or going all out and buying you a soda?"

Cold resentment made Midge's voice quietly firm as she answered, "We're going to a concert, one of the regular series at the high school. It's a symphony orchestra this time."

"Big deal!" Sandra said. "I'm really impressed!" A note of impatience sharpened her voice, "Honestly, Midge, I don't know what's getting into you! You're so queer lately. What will the kids think?"

"I don't care!" Midge said hotly, although this wasn't entirely true. She did care. She wanted the crowd to think well of her, she wanted to continue to be included in it. But at the same time, she wanted to be herself, to retain some freedom of choice. Uncertainty gnawed at her; she felt pulled two ways.

"Don't you really?" Sandra asked, her tone cool.

"Oh, of course I do," Midge admitted unhappily. "You know I care what they think."

"Then break your date tonight," Sandra said flatly. "After all, a concert!"

"No," Midge told her, "I won't. I happen to like Hans. I wouldn't hurt him for the world. Anyway," she admitted, "I doubt that my folks would let me go to that night club."

"Why not, for heaven's sake? We're only going to dance. The kids are all too young to be served liquor."

"Even so," Midge said. She didn't add that her parents were convinced that a crowd of teen-agers, driving long distances in packed cars late at night, were simply asking for trouble.

Sandra's sigh was exasperated. "Oh, all right, if you're going to be that way! But you'd better not turn the crowd down too often, or you'll find yourself not getting asked."

"I know," Midge said, "but I can't help it."

She had a very pleasant evening with Hans. Sitting in the darkened auditorium, feeling the surge and swell of the magnificent music all about, Midge experienced a curious sensation, but one she had known many times before. It was as though the music served to release her imagination, so that it soared and swooped, touching on strange things and never-visited places. She was in a garden in far-off Araby for a while, then she watched great armies clashing on a broad plain outside a walled city, and still later she seemed to see tiny, bright-colored birds darting from branch to branch in a lush tropical jungle.

When the lights went up during intermission, she glimpsed on Hans's face the same dreamy, bemused look that she felt must mark her own. And she asked, "Does music like that make you feel as if you are different people in all sorts of strange faraway places, as if you're—outside yourself?"

Although she hadn't found exactly the right words, he seemed to understand. "I feel drunk with beauty," he answered gravely. "Noble thoughts, high ambitions, these bear me up and away into a better world. Is it so with you too?"

Midge nodded, smiling. It was definitely so with her too. But she hadn't often found someone to whom she could admit it, someone who wouldn't find it amusing or silly.

People milled about them, leaving their seats to go out into the corridor and stretch their legs, returning to their places once more, speaking to friends, discussing the concert. But Midge and Hans seemed to be shut off in a small private world of their own, in which they could sit quietly, their shoulders touching, a deep kinship of the spirit binding them together. When they felt like speaking, they spoke. But their silences were equally companionable. And when the lights dimmed once more and the crowd quieted and the orchestra members lifted their instruments, awaiting the signal of the leader, Midge found her hand held close in that of Hans. And this time, when the swelling music bore them on its crest to a dream world of their own imagining, they seemed to go together.

Later Midge decided against the soda Hans politely offered to buy her at Joe's Grill. "It's not that I'm not hungry," she admitted with a faint smile, "but I just can't bear the thought of that blaring jukebox after what we've been hearing."

"My own feeling exactly," Hans gave her elbow a little squeeze. "But I, too, am starving. What would you suggest we do?"

"Let's go raid the refrigerator at my house," Midge said. "There's always something there."

This time there proved to be leftover turkey, and Midge and Hans concocted generous sandwiches which they ate with olives and chocolate milk, rounding off the whole with wedges of angel-food cake left from dinner.

"This is much better than Joe's Grill," Hans said, as they lingered over their repast at the kitchen table. "I like your house. It is the same as your family, warm and friendly."

"It's pretty old and sort of inconvenient," Midge admitted, "but we like it. I've lived here ever since I was born."

"You have roots," Hans nodded, helping himself to another olive. "Not many people have, any more. They drift about like gypsies—where their jobs take them, where their curiosity draws them, sometimes just from house to house for the sake of something newer and with more conveniences. But roots are better."

"Maybe it only means we're in a rut," Midge said, more for the sake of argument than because she actually thought so.

"No," Hans shook his head decisively, "this is not true of you or your family. To be in a rut is not a matter of staying in one place, but of having narrow ideas. You have a curious, questioning mind. You don't merely want to know how things are, you ask why they are so. You read history, not only as much as is assigned in school, but more widely, because you are interested in what mankind has been in the past."

"You make me sound like a brain," Midge said wryly.

"This is bad?" Hans frowned. "I mean it as a compliment."

"I know, and I appreciate it," Midge said. "It's just that, at school, to be considered a brain is to be thought—well, a little strange and different."

"Such a passion for sameness, for mediocrity, you Americans have developed." Hans shook his head wonderingly. "To be average seems to be your goal. Yet in our world today minds and spirits far above average are desperately needed. These we must develop merely in order to survive. Do you not agree?"

As they talked on, Midge was aware that she had not talked so seriously with a boy before, though some of the discussions between Tom Brooks and her last summer might have approached it. She found herself wishing that Tom and Hans could meet. She felt sure they'd like each other. And they would find stimulation in an exchange of ideas, such as was going on between Hans and her right now. She, too, found it exciting. How stereotyped and dull, how repetitive, most of the talk the crowd indulged in seemed by comparison. Of course, she reminded herself loyally, no one wanted to be serious all the time. Still, Sandra and the others were practically never serious; they made fun of everything. Life was a big fat laugh, and even remotely to consider it otherwise was to risk being looked on as an oddball.

The crowd would be utterly convulsed if they could hear Hans and her talking right now! Midge's cheeks grew hot with embarrassment just to think of it. But whether her discomfiture was due to her own unwillingness to seem funny, or whether it grew out of her sudden, sharp resentment at the idea of anyone's jeering at Hans, she wasn't quite sure.

With Tobey's and Brose's departure and the start of classes Midge was caught up in her customary routine. School and its attendant homework, club meetings, an occasional evening spent with Hans or out on a date arranged by Sandra, these activities kept her busy. She managed to find time to write now and then to Tom and Judy, and she thoroughly enjoyed the letters she got in return. Judy was happily settled in her new home and quite as busy as Midge with a whole new circle of friends. Tom still dwelt wistfully on the fun they'd had last summer, and he wrote hopefully of the possibility of getting together again sometime in the future. Midge, too, hoped that they could do this. But she spent no time in brooding about it.

Despite Sandra's continued opposition, Midge tried to get better acquainted with Tricia Farnham. The little time she had spent in her company had convinced Midge that they were congenial. Talking with Tricia was almost like talking with Judy again. Midge sensed in her the same definiteness of viewpoint, the same frank statement of opinion that she had so enjoyed when she and Judy used to hash everything over together. If it hadn't been for the spector of suspicion that Sandra's confidences concerning Tricia had left to haunt Midge's thoughts, she would have felt herself irresistibly drawn to the other girl. But enough of an element of doubt remained so that she was just a little cautious in their relationship. And apparently Tricia sensed this faint touch of aloofness and matched it with an understandable hesitancy of her own, so that their acquaintanceship, though warm enough on the surface, did not deepen into a real friendship.

Whenever Sandra saw Midge and Tricia walking casually down a corridor together at school or talking as they emerged from a class, she managed, the next time she and Midge were alone, to drop some hint as to Tricia's duplicity, her undependability.

"Oh, she can be very sweet to your face," Sandra warned. "But don't turn your back on her for a minute!"

"What did she do to you exactly?" Midge asked. "I know you said she worked on Terry and got him away from you. But could she do that unless he was willing?"

116

"Don't be naïve!" Sandra admonished. "I told you she lied about me and then, when Terry and I broke up, she was just waiting with open arms to grab him."

"Yes, and you told me they broke up right afterward, as soon as he found out what she was really like. But they're sure back together again now, and everything seems fine."

Sandra shrugged. "I have no idea how she managed that. Probably more lies. She's so good at them."

"But she doesn't seem that way," Midge argued. "She doesn't seem like that at all."

"Okay," Sandra said. "Find out for yourself if you must. But don't say I didn't warn you. I figure that's the least a friend can do."

Midge supposed Sandra was right. She must be. After all, Sandra had known Tricia much more intimately than she did. And yet there seemed to be a small, stubborn core of resistance deep within Midge that Sandra's words, positive as they were, couldn't entirely melt.

"I appreciate it, Sandra. Really, I do," Midge told her.

Sandra smiled at her, that warm, wide smile that was so winning, so irresistible. "That's all right," she answered, laying her hand companionably on Midge's arm for a moment. "I just don't want you to get burned, the way I did. I happen to like you too well for that."

CHAPTER 13

Bob Raises Some Questions

One of the most popular dances of the year at Edgewood High was the Sweater Hop, traditionally held in early December. The boys liked it because it was so informal. And the girls liked it because a boy, well aware of the modest outlay of cash required, was more likely to invite a girl to it than to some of the more lavish dances. The Heart Hop and the Junior and Senior Proms took a much heavier financial toll. For these, corsages were expected, plus the price of renting a tux for the large majority not fortunate enough to own one, plus something rather special in the way of after-dance food and entertainment. But all that was needed for the Sweater Hop was a new, or at least presentable, sweater, and the negligible price of a pair of tickets. And so it was generally very well attended.

However, even before the Thanksgiving weekend

was over, Midge had begun to feel worried about her chances of being invited to the Hop. With Sandra's impatience mounting over her unwillingness to snub Tricia Farnham, it seemed unlikely she would be moved to include Midge in a double date. And the fact that Hans hadn't so much as mentioned the affair made Midge suspect that a lack of confidence in his ability to dance American-style was making him shy away from a repetition of his inadequacy at the Sophomore Mixer.

For the first time Midge was a little tempted to fall back on that ridiculous promise of Bob's, made away back last summer, to take her to any school affair for which she didn't have a more appealing invitation. But how, she wondered, would you go about hinting to even as old a friend as Bob that you might be forced to consider him as a last resort? It certainly wouldn't be flattering, and it would be a hard blow for one's own pride to take as well.

She kept hoping against hope that Sandra would come through with an offer to have Ben line up someone for her. But Sandra simply ignored the prospect of the Hop, although she and Midge spent quite a bit of time together as usual, while Midge did the lion's share of their homework. The thought occurred to Midge that Sandra might be deliberately inflicting punishment on her for her rebellion in the matter of Tricia and the occasional evenings she spent with Hans. And this suspicion made her, too, stubbornly refrain from mentioning the Sweater Hop. If Sandra wanted to be that way, let her, Midge thought! On the other hand, if her nagging suspicion was incorrect and Sandra's avoidance of the subject purely accidental, she still wasn't going to be the one to bring it up. After all, there were limits to how far she'd go to get a date. She certainly didn't mean to beg Sandra to fix something up for her!

As the day of the dance drew nearer, Midge's attitude grew fatalistically resigned. If she wasn't going to get to go to the Hop, she wasn't—that was all there was to it. She'd live. Then one day after school, as she was walking home, Bob's 1919 Marmon drew up impressively at the curb and Bob himself, sitting behind the wheel, called to her, "Hey, Midge! Want a lift?"

"You're driving!" Midge exclaimed in surprise. As she walked toward the car, she did a rapid mental calculation. "That's right, you had a birthday, didn't you? Sorry I forgot it."

"That's okay. I'll forget yours," Bob grinned, holding the door hospitably open for her to climb in. "I've got my driver's license, too, so it's all legal."

"Congratulations," Midge said. "How does it feel to be so old?"

"Just great," Bob told her. "I've been waiting a long time."

"No more than sixteen years," Midge laughed.

It was like old times, kidding with Bob. Maybe, she thought, if she handled it very carefully, she could finagle things so he'd ask her to the Sweater Hop without too great damage to either his pride or hers.

"How come you're not following the Queen around?" Bob asked. "She let you have a day off?"

"Oh, honestly!" Midge said. "Do you take lessons in being objectionable, or does it just come naturally?"

"It's a gift," Bob told her. "Not everyone brings it out in me, though. You're just lucky."

"I can think of better words to describe it," she said.

"Speaking of words," Bob drawled, "how are you doing with Sandra's English these days? Getting good marks for her?"

"Just what is that supposed to mean?" Midge asked icily.

"Oh, come on, this is old Bob, remember? You can be honest with me! You know you're doing most of her schoolwork, and not just in English, either."

"I seem to recall having helped you with yours on occasion," Midge reminded, feeling anger rise in her. But, in a way, it was foolish to get so mad when Bob was only saying things she had so often thought.

"Helping's one thing and doing it all for someone is another," Bob argued.

"How do you know so much about it—or think you do?"

"Are you honestly denying it?" Bob asked, and Midge could only stare at him, her eyes wide with the sudden realization that she couldn't actually say he was wrong. "You see?" Bob's tone was more gentle. "You know it's true, only you can't bear to come right out and admit it. Remember," he asked then, "when we were talking about Sandra a long time back and you said she was just being friendly because she liked you and I said she must want something from you?"

Midge remembered. "Yes, but——"

"Now," Bob broke in, "I'm pretty sure just what it is she wants. A stooge to do her studying for her, so she can get by without any work. And you're it, you've been elected. Tricia used to have the job, but she got fed up and quit."

"Did she tell you so?" Midge demanded.

"No, Terry did," Bob explained. "He was right there and saw it all happening. Then, when Tricia finally rebelled, he took her side in it and that's when he and Sandra broke up."

"It wasn't that way at all," Midge said flatly. "You've only heard their story. But Sandra says Tricia was determined to get Terry away from her. She told him all sorts of fantastic lies about Sandra and then——"

"I don't believe that," Bob interrupted. "You know Tricia well enough to be sure she wouldn't tell lies."

"Neither would Sandra," Midge insisted loyally.

They had reached the Heydon house now, and Bob braked the car to a halt on the drive, shaking his head. "How can you be so stupid as not to see through her? You're like a poor snake," he went on disgustedly, "being charmed by a snake charmer. You haven't any mind of your own where Sandra's concerned. But what I don't get is why—why? She's a snob and a dope and she's only taking advantage of you by having you do all her work and then paying you back with a few crumbs—an in with that stuck-up crowd of hers and a date now and then."

"You don't know what you're talking about!" Midge said hotly. She was so angry, so stirred up, she felt as though she might burst into tears any minute. And she would not cry in front of Bob. She wouldn't give him the satisfaction. She managed a choked, "You make me sick!" as she got the door open, jumped down from the queer, high running board, and hurried into the house. The thought that only a little while earlier she had been toying with the idea of trying to get Bob to ask her to the Sweater Hop had been erased from her mind entirely.

She wished she could as easily dismiss some of the disturbing ideas their talk had implanted. But the things Bob had said about Sandra just couldn't be true! As a friend of Terry's and so of Tricia's, he'd naturally share their very biased viewpoint. Sandra had told Midge long ago that Tricia was two-faced and not to be trusted, that she had misrepresented the situation between Sandra and her in order to put the best light possible on her own conduct.

A troubling memory stirred in Midge. It wasn't Tricia who had supplied Bob with the details, it was Terry. Did that indicate that Terry, also, was not to be believed? Or had his fondness for Tricia misled him into accepting everything she told him as true and so doing Sandra a grave injustice? Midge's thoughts kept going around and around in circles, getting nowhere. How could you know the truth about something that had happened away back last year? Naturally whoever told you about it would be influenced by whatever her part had been in the whole ugly affair.

"Mom, you home?" Midge called tentatively, although the unbroken quiet of the house made her fairly certain it was empty. This was her mother's bridge-club day, she remembered then, which meant Mom probably wouldn't be home till five or later.

Okay, Midge thought, so I'll get dinner. That'll give me enough to do to keep me from thinking!

She tied one of Mom's aprons around her and switched on the kitchen radio for company. In the refrigerator she found a meat loaf all ready to bake. Midge scrubbed potatoes and put them and the meat into the oven. She even prepared a package of gingerbread mix for dessert and concocted a fairly elaborate salad. But despite her dogged activity and the radio's blaring distraction, her mind kept on twisting and turning. And deep within her a small voice she didn't want to listen to said clearly, "You feel Sandra's taking advantage of you in this homework business. So how can you be so sure she didn't go through the same routine with Tricia? Maybe sometime you'll reach a point where you get fed up, too, and tell her off. And then, besides getting you out of the crowd, she may concoct some fantastic story about you."

"She won't!" Midge told the voice positively. "I'm sure of it! I may just be imagining I'm doing more than my share of our homework. And Bob doesn't know a thing about it really. He just got this notion from what Terry told him. Sometime, when I get to know Tricia better, maybe I'll come right out and ask her why she and Sandra stopped being friends."

"If," the annoying small voice argued, "you ever do

124

get to know Tricia better. Sandra's done a first-rate job of keeping that from happening so far."

"She hasn't!" Midge denied. "It's—just one of those things, not her doing at all. Why blame her because we've happened to be double dating the few times Bob's suggested going out with Tricia and Terry? And I've seen quite a bit of Tricia around school. We're perfectly friendly."

"Oh, school!" the inner voice hooted. "There's never much chance to talk there. Why don't you call Tricia up sometime, make a friendly gesture? Unless, that is, you're afraid of getting better acquainted."

"All right, I will!" Midge's decision was so sudden and positive that for a moment it almost seemed as though she had said the words aloud. But she hadn't actually started talking to herself yet, she thought wryly. She hadn't cracked up to that extent.

However, she found herself moving purposefully toward the phone in the hall and sliding the directory out of its drawer in the stand in order to look up the Farnhams' number. But before she had reached the F's, the phone rang and Midge jumped, so shrill and near was its sound. Wouldn't it be strange if it were Tricia calling her?

But the voice that reached her ear was much deeper than Tricia's. "Midge? This is Hans."

"Oh, yes," Midge said, a curious sensation of relief flooding through her, almost as though she had been granted a reprieve from some sort of punishment. "How are you, Hans?"

"Very well, thank you." A faint undertone of amusement sounded through the polite words.

It had been, Midge realized, a rather stupid question on her part. After all, she had seen him only a few hours ago in Chemistry. Unless he had suffered some sort of accident on his way home from school, he was pretty sure to be all right.

She rushed into vivacious conversation, trying to cover up the ineptitude of her initial remark. "You'll never guess what I've been doing! In fact, I'll bet you didn't even realize I could do it!"

"What is that?" Hans queried.

"Getting dinner," Midge informed him. "I just suddenly felt like doing my good deed for the day and since this is my mother's afternoon to play bridge, I thought I'd surprise her by having dinner all ready by the time she gets home. Wasn't that sweet of me? Do you suppose she'll appreciate it?"

"I imagine she will," Hans said agreeably. He hesitated briefly and when he continued his voice had assumed a questioning, more serious note. "Midge, what's the matter?"

His perception made her eyes mist suddenly. And she asked, "Why do you think anything is? Because I don't usually babble quite so senselessly?"

"It's not that," he said in the same sympathetic tone. "But—your manner doesn't seem quite natural. I wondered if perhaps you were trying to hide some disappointment, or worry."

"You must be psychic," Midge told him with a wry little laugh. "But it's nothing I can talk about—

126

just a sort of mood, I guess. Do you ever get them
—moods, I mean?"

"Ah, yes," Hans said. "Moods when I feel on top
of the world. And others when it seems to rest on my
shoulders and weigh me down. Often they are quite
without cause."

"Mine is pretty much like that too," Midge said.
And she must have begun to sound more like herself,
because Hans let the matter drop and went on to tell
her the reason for his call.

"Are you going to this dance, this Sweater Hop, next
week?" he asked.

"Why, no." Her heart began to hurry just a little.

"Then would you do me the honor to go with me?"
Hans asked with his odd, but rather endearing, touch
of Old-World formality. "You see, I have been prac-
ticing my dancing. Mrs. Armstrong has been so kind
as to help me. I waited to invite you," he admitted
with a humility that touched Midge, "so that if you
wished to go with someone more exciting and—I think
the word is 'smooth'—then a commitment to me
wouldn't stand in your way."

"Don't talk like that," Midge told him, her voice a
trifle husky. "I'd love to go to the Hop with you,
Hans." Then she added, rather surprised to discover
that it was quite true, "I can't think of anyone else
I'd rather go with."

CHAPTER 14

The Sweater Hop

The next time Midge saw Bob, he apologized. True, he rather spoiled things by winding up with, "After all, it's your own affair if you want to go on letting Sandra take advantage of you." This naturally tended to detract from the satisfaction Midge felt at hearing him say he was sorry. Still, an apology was an apology, and there seemed no good reason not to accept it.

Bob, who had cornered her near her locker, proceeded to walk down the corridor with her on the way to their next classes. And as they walked, he inquired flatly, "You going to the Hop?"

"Yes." Midge felt a small thrust of pleasure because she didn't have to say just the opposite. "Are you?"

"I don't know," Bob admitted. He went on then with the complete candor of old friendship, "I've been sort of holding off, waiting to see whether you wanted me to take you. If you don't, though, maybe I'll ask Jen Travers."

128

"Well, you'd better ask her pretty soon!" Midge scolded. After all, the Hop was only a few days off. "You didn't have to wait around for me! Any time you want to ask someone else to anything, for creep's sake, ask her!"

"Yeah, but a promise is a promise," Bob said. "And I told you——"

"So un-tell me!" Midge interrupted. "I don't intend to hold you to such a crazy promise. You're free to date anyone you want to any time." Having established that fact once and for all, she continued in a milder tone, "I didn't even know you were interested in Jen."

Bob blushed to the roots of his stubby brown hair. "Who says I'm interested?" he demanded. "Just because you ask a girl to a dance doesn't mean you care a hoot about her!"

"Of course not," Midge agreed.

"It's just that I figured I'd ask someone so we could double with Terry and Tricia. And Jen's not as revolting as some of the girls around. She's got a *little* sense."

"Sure, she has," Midge agreed. "She's cute, too."

"Cute?" Bob queried, frowning. "You think so?" Midge nodded.

"D'you suppose she'll go with me?"

"You'll never know if you don't ask," Midge pointed out. "I expect she will—unless you've fooled around and waited so late that she already has a date."

"I'll ask her this afternoon," Bob said, with the same dogged determination he had shown when they were in fifth grade and he was setting his sights on some more juvenile objective.

"You do that," Midge egged him on. "I'll keep my fingers crossed for you."

"It's not that important," Bob's tone altered to one of aloof detachment. Suddenly he thought to ask, "By the way, whom are you going with?" When Midge told him, he nodded in approval. "Good! I was afraid Sandra had fixed you up with some goon."

"For your information——" Midge began heatedly.

But Bob broke in, his manner placating, "Okay, okay! So long as it's Hans you're going with, let's not have another hassle. Got to take off now, or I'll be late for Math. See you."

What a sneaky way to have the last word, Midge thought, staring after him with a faint smile as he loped off.

Sandra's reaction when she learned that Midge was going to the Sweater Hop with Hans was just the opposite of Bob's. She was incensed. "Why didn't you tell me you needed a date? I'd have had Ben get someone for you—someone who'd fit into the crowd, someone acceptable."

"Hans is acceptable to me," Midge told her quietly. "Isn't that the important thing?" She went on then, before Sandra could answer, "I'm getting a little fed up on the idea of letting the crowd do my thinking for me, decide whether someone's okay for me to date or not. After all, the crowd doesn't own me."

"That's right," Sandra agreed. She stared at Midge, her dark eyes narrowed, "But you seem to enjoy the

130

privilege of being a part of it. And you can't have that without accepting the crowd's standards as to who's okay and who isn't. If you go to the Hop with Hans, they'll simply ignore you——"

"I don't care!" Midge broke in, her eyes bright with indignation. "I'll ignore them right back! If you're so fussy about whom I go with, you should have got me a date with someone else before Hans asked me. There was plenty of time."

"I suppose it is partly my fault," Sandra nodded. "I should have found out whether you wanted me to have Ben line up someone for you. But you've been turning me down a lot lately."

"Only when I had something else planned first," Midge assured her. "You know I appreciate your getting dates for me."

"Do you?" Sandra asked. "Sometimes I wonder."

"Of course I do," Midge said. "It's just that I don't like to beg you to do it. I'm not that desperate!"

Sandra smiled gently. "There's no use flipping about it. I'm only trying to help." It was hard to hold out against her charm when she turned it on full force, as she proceeded to do now. She soothed Midge, "I just don't want you to risk your place in the crowd till you're more firmly established. If you keep on dating outsiders——" her slight shrug was eloquent. "I wouldn't interfere if we weren't friends, if I didn't like you so well."

Her air was sweetly reasonable, her smile winning. Midge felt the edges of her anger begin to soften. She heard herself explaining, almost unwillingly, "I was afraid I wasn't going to get to the Hop at all."

"I know," Sandra nodded. "I'm not blaming you for going with Hans, although I'm afraid you won't have much fun. But promise me one thing, will you?"

"What?" Midge queried.

"Promise me," Sandra said, "not to get involved with anyone for the Saturday night before Christmas. That's when the big holiday dance at the country club will be held and our whole crowd's going. I'll get you a date with someone extra-special. And then afterward we'll all go to my house for a party. Okay?"

"Oh, yes," Midge breathed, her face lighting and her heart beating fast with anticipation at the exciting prospect. "That would be wonderful!"

Sandra's glance was thoughtful. After a moment she asked, "Would you like to go with Pete Lovejoy?"

"Pete Lovejoy?" Midge's tone was incredulous. Pete was a tall, dark-haired junior, new at Edgewood this year, but a big favorite with the crowd because of his devil-may-care attractiveness and his impressive prowess on the football team during the season just past. "You're kidding!"

"No, I'm not," Sandra denied. "Ben says Pete's had his eye on you for a long time. I'm sure we could fix it up."

"But I've hardly talked to him at all!" Midge was finding it hard to catch her breath.

"Then a date for the Christmas dance will give you a good chance to get acquainted," Sandra smiled knowingly. "Shall I see what I can do?"

"Gee, will you?" Midge's tone was abjectly grateful.

A dance at the country club, a possible date with Pete Lovejoy, and a party afterward at Sandra's house —it all added up to a night to dream about, a prospect almost too good to be true. How had she ever been so lucky, Midge wondered, as to find a friend like Sandra?

Under the circumstances, the Sweater Hop was almost bound to seem diminished in importance, Midge supposed. Still, she was determined to let no hint of this mar the occasion, either for Hans or herself. Hans's own lively enthusiasm made this easy to live up to. Midge's spirits rose to match his from the moment when she came downstairs to find him talking easily with her parents in the living room while he waited for her.

"I'm sorry to be late," she apologized.

But Hans, rising to his feet politely, assured her, "You are not. I was early." He smiled then, admitting, "I guess I was just anxious for the evening to begin."

"So am I," Midge told him, smiling, too, feeling her heart quicken.

"How lovely you look!" Hans said right in front of her parents, not waiting until they were alone outside, as an American boy more likely would have done. His blue gaze rested in frank approval on Midge's matching turquoise sweater and pleated skirt, her hair brushed into a soft swirl of bangs across her forehead.

"Why, thanks," Midge murmured, feeling color

creep across her cheeks, aware of her parents' natural enjoyment of the moment, but not minding, really. "You look very nice too."

"My sweater is suitable?" Hans glanced down at his rust-colored pullover, which went very well with his dark-brown slacks. His rueful smile reminded Midge that he was probably remembering the night of the Sophomore Mixer, when his neat dark suit and white shirt and tie had set him apart from all the other, more casually dressed, males.

"Oh, yes," Midge assured him. "It's very nice."

Her father, unaware of the undercurrents of meaning beneath their spoken words, remarked, "Hans was just telling us that families who put up exchange students are told not to let them drive their cars. I didn't realize that."

"It is because of the problems which arise in case of an accident," Hans explained. "Matters of insurance and responsibility become most complex when natives of foreign countries are involved. I don't mind, really," he smiled, "so long as I am fortunate enough to find a girl who will walk with me."

"Henry," Mom said, on what Midge felt sure was a helpful impulse, "you could drive them to school, couldn't you?"

"Of course," Dad agreed without a moment's hesitation. "I'll be glad to." He braced his hands on the arms of his chair, as if to push himself up out of its comfortable depths.

Midge died a thousand deaths. It would seem so dreadfully junior-high to be driven to a dance by your

134

parents! Mom and Dad weren't aware of that, of course. Nor could Hans, in all likelihood, sense how much she'd rather walk.

His glance sought hers for only a second, however, before he turned to smile at her father and say, "You are very kind, but I don't think either of us minds walking."

"Oh, we don't!" Midge exclaimed gratefully. "It isn't as if it were a formal dance, where I'd be wearing heels. And the school's only a few blocks. I'd really like to walk!"

Her parents didn't press the point. But not until Midge and Hans were in the street outside, with the chill moonlight shining down on them through the leafless branches of trees, did she breathe entirely easily.

"You were worried," Hans remarked with that curiously deep perception Midge had sensed in him before. "You feared I would accept your parents' kind offer to take us in their car to the dance." He chuckled. "Mr. Armstrong made a like offer, but I declined that too. You see, I am—as you say—catching on."

They laughed together, walking arm in arm along the empty street. And Midge admitted ruefully, "I was scared for a minute. It seems so terribly juvenile to be taken places by your parents."

"I can see that," Hans nodded. "And we must seem old at all costs, is that not true?"

"Sometimes," Midge accused, "I have the feeling you're making fun of me, that you find me—a little absurd."

"I find you charming," Hans told her, his voice quite grave. "Beautiful, kind, friendly, good—all these things I find you as well. And if I tease, it is only because I like you so well and between friends a little teasing is permitted, is it not?" He gave her gloved hand a firm squeeze and did not relinquish it as they walked on. "Now I have embarrassed you, I fear."

"I'm—flattered," Midge said, her voice low and a bit uncertain. "I just don't quite know what to say when you talk that way."

"You could say," Hans told her, "that you like me, too. I should like so well to hear that."

"I do like you," Midge said, touched by his sincerity, by the note almost of yearning in his voice. "I'm glad we're friends, that we can talk to each other about serious things, our thoughts, our feelings, the way we feel about life. And still, we can laugh together, too, and have fun."

Hans nodded. "That's what friends are," he told her, "people who can be gay together or serious, as the occasion demands, who understand and respect each other's ideas, who may differ, but do not quarrel, because of the bond that draws them together." He stopped speaking as the lighted façade of the high school loomed before them, looking larger and more impressive in the setting of darkness. "We are here already," he said, surprised. "As always, when we walk and talk, the time seems too short."

Midge nodded in agreement as they went up the stairs. Inside they were engulfed in a tide of fellow students, shedding coats at the improvised checkroom, making their way toward the brightly decorated gym. Music blared at them and Hans said, "I do not feel quite so much at a loss when I hear that beat. But you will have to make allowances even yet."

Actually, though, he danced very well. Not only had Mrs. Armstrong taught him the rudiments of rock and roll, she must also have convinced him, Midge suspected, that in America one did not whirl quite so madly in the waltzes. "You're doing wonderfully," Midge assured him. And she was curious enough to ask, "How does Mrs. Armstrong know so much about the newer dances?"

"She learned from her children, she told me, when they were in high school," Hans smiled. "Lucky for me, was it not?"

During the course of the evening Midge saw little of Sandra and the rest of the crowd. Beyond the most casual of hellos, they ignored her, just as Sandra had warned they would. Several times Midge glimpsed them laughing together in a tight little clump, appearing to be having a much better time than anyone else. Were the girls actually among the prettiest in the big room, were the boys more attractive and wittily assured than anyone else? Or was this simply an impression they sought to give, Midge wondered, so that everyone outside their magic circle would feel left out, as though they were missing something?

But there were countless other cliques around school, all undoubtedly considering themselves equally exclusive. It was almost like children playing games, gathering a favored few intimates about them, shutting

137

the rest out. When you got right down to it, was it really of earth-shaking importance one way or the other?

The idea so startled Midge that she felt she had to give it further serious consideration. But not right now, not tonight, when she was having so much fun simply being with Hans, when they were both enjoying the gaiety and excitement of the dance to the fullest. She was glad she had come with him, no matter what Sandra thought about it, or what she said.

Bob danced past with auburn-haired Jen Travers. They smiled and spoke to Midge and Hans, as did Tricia and Terry a moment later. And Tricia suggested, "Have refreshments with us during intermission," her tone warm and friendly.

"We'd love to, wouldn't we, Hans?" Midge agreed.

"Of course," Hans nodded, smiling.

So, let the crowd ignore her, Midge thought, happily aware of Hans's arm about her, his breath stirring the hair at her temple as he spoke. She'd survive. With a minimum of effort she dismissed all thought of Sandra and the others from her mind and concentrated her full attention on her partner.

CHAPTER 15

An Exciting Invitation

On Monday after the Sweater Hop Midge and Sandra were doing their homework together in Sandra's bedroom. Sandra, who was lying across the bed with a book she had scarcely glanced at in one hand, remarked, "I saw you eating with Tricia and Terry the other night. Did she say anything about me?"

Midge glanced up with a faint frown from the Math problems she was working out for both of them. "No, she never talks about you—at least, not to me."

"She will," Sandra drawled, "when she feels she knows you well enough."

"Why do you think so?" Midge queried. "We're pretty good friends now and she's never even mentioned your name. In fact, you seem much more prone to talk about her."

"I have a right to," Sandra said, her dark glance hard, "after the way she treated me."

"Is it true," Midge couldn't resist asking, since, after

all, Sandra herself had brought up the subject, "that she used to do a lot of your homework for you?"

"She *has* been telling you lies!" Sandra accused hotly.

"No," Midge shook her head, "that's something I heard from Bob Pierson. And it was Terry who told him."

"Oh, Terry!" Sandra said scathingly. "Tricia's got him so completely under her thumb, she can convince him of anything. Simply anything at all!"

"But she did help you with your homework?"

"We did it together," Sandra's tone was soft now, with a note of hurt beneath it. "Lots of friends do that. There's nothing wrong about it." She asked then, her dark eyes wide and pleading, "Do you feel I'm taking advantage of you?"

"It sometimes seems to me," Midge said dryly, "that I do rather more than my share."

"But that's just because everything comes so easily for you," Sandra reminded. "And stuff like that——" she pointed at the page of problems Midge was in the midst of, "well, wouldn't it be stupid for us both to work them all out, when one can do it?"

Midge stared at her for a moment. "But you aren't learning anything," she pointed out, "when I do it all. You won't be able to rationalize your way out of exams."

"Don't worry your head about them," Sandra said airily.

Midge had a pretty strong hunch what she meant. She knew that a good deal of cheating went on at

140

school. And she didn't doubt that Sandra would work things out some way so that she'd achieve a passing grade, whether by fair means or foul. The idea sickened Midge. Why couldn't kids who sneaked the answers into class, in one ingenious way or another, realize that they were really only cheating themselves out of knowledge they might someday wish they had?

She told Sandra, "I think you're being foolish. And if you're counting on me to help you with exams——"

"I'm not," Sandra broke in. "I know that awful conscience of yours. Why, you felt guilty over writing a little measly theme for me. But I like you just the same."

"Gee, thanks," Midge said.

"In fact," Sandra went on, smiling, "I've done you a big fat favor. So don't imagine our helping each other is all one-sided."

"What sort of favor?" Midge's tone was doubtful.

"Got you a date for the Christmas dance," Sandra informed her, "with none other than Pete Lovejoy."

Midge could only sit staring, her heart beating in heavy thumps, hardly able to believe what Sandra was saying. All thought of Tricia, of Hans, of homework and large moral issues was wiped from her mind. Pete filled it, threatened to burst it. Pete, larger than life, his dark hair curlier than ever, his black eyes lighted with laughing fire, his mouth curved in such an attractive grin Midge could scarcely bear the thought of it.

"You mean—" she managed to gulp, "it's all set?"

"Of course," Sandra nodded. "I told you I'd have

141

Ben fix it up. He says Pete's very pleased. He thinks you're cute."

"Did he tell Ben that?" Midge demanded, feeling giddy and giggly with excitement. "Did he actually say he thought I was cute, or are you just making that up?"

"He told Ben so," Sandra said. "When Ben first brought up the subject of doubling, Pete didn't seem too interested. Then when Ben mentioned your name, Pete's attitude changed and he said he'd like to go with us. So—you see?"

"I can't believe it," Midge reiterated.

Why should anyone so terrific as Pete Lovejoy be remotely interested in her? She pried from Sandra every detail the other girl knew of the conversation between Pete and Ben. Still, Midge couldn't understand her good fortune. A boy so popular, so spectacularly attractive as Pete, would have his pick of girls. Of course, Midge reminded herself, the country club dance was a private affair. If he didn't go as a guest of someone like Sandra, whose parents were members, he might not get to go at all. Even so, it was terribly flattering that he was willing to take her.

She finished off the Math assignment in a happy daze and was pleasantly surprised to find that her answers checked out correctly. She let Sandra copy her paper, not feeling as guilty about this as usual. When they had finished their homework, Sandra phoned Ben and the two of them drove Midge home.

She couldn't resist asking Ben, "You're sure Pete's willing to take me to the Christmas dance? You didn't

142

twist his arm or anything?"

"How could I?" Ben grinned in his lordly superior manner. "He's bigger than I."

"But he didn't seem to mind?" Midge pressed anxiously.

Ben asked Sandra, "What's she got, an inferiority complex or something?" He addressed Midge then, "No, kid, he's all for it. He'll probably call you, or say something about it at school. I told him to check with you what color dress you'll be wearing, so he'll know about a corsage and all that jazz."

Midge scarcely heard any of the ensuing conversation between Sandra and Ben. When they let her out at her house and drove off into the gathering dusk, she seemed to float along several inches above the sidewalk. She wasn't at all conscious of going through the motions of walking, setting one foot down before the other. Somewhere far back in her mind a sort of lilting echo kept repeating over and over, "You're going to have a date with Pete Lovejoy, Pete Lovejoy, Pete Lovejoy."

Midge let herself into the house quietly, then stood for an ecstatic moment leaning against the door, her eyes closed. An enticing aroma of apple pie baking tickled her nostrils, but she was too caught up in the enchantment of the wonderful thing that had happened to be more than vaguely aware of such mundane things as dessert. In fact, she didn't feel as if she would ever need to eat again. After a moment she opened her eyes and looked around the familiar hall. The stairs with their polished railing and white-painted, carpeted treads, the rug that was beginning to show faint signs of wear, the wallpaper with its tiny floral pattern in shades of beige and apricot and turquoise—everything looked brighter and clearer somehow, as though Midge's perceptions had been sharpened, her awareness of detail increased. She seemed to see more clearly, feel more strongly, be more alive.

And suddenly she knew a mounting need to share with someone the wonderful, incredible thing that had happened to her. Otherwise, Midge felt, she might simply burst and fly in all directions, like an over-inflated balloon.

"Mom," she called, her tone demanding, "where are you?"

"Out here," her mother answered from the kitchen. "I didn't hear you come in."

Midge tossed her books onto the bottom step and danced out to the kitchen, where she caught her mother around the waist in a bear hug and planted a happy kiss on her cheek before releasing her. "Guess what happened!"

"Something wonderful, it's obvious," Mom smiled.

"Think of the most absolutely terrific thing that could possibly happen," Midge instructed. "Then multiply it by ten. And you still wouldn't be anywhere near it!"

"Well, tell me," Mom said, "before I die of curiosity."

Midge crossed her arms, hugging herself ecstatically. "Pete Lovejoy," she said slowly, savoring each word to the very fullest, "is going to take me to the Christmas

144

dance. Imagine!"

A faint frown wrinkled Mom's brow, even while her lips still retained a trace of a smile. "The Christmas dance sounds exciting," she admitted. "But who is Pete Lovejoy?"

"Oh, Mother!" Midge said accusingly. "You must have heard of Pete Lovejoy, or read about him in the paper when the football season was on, or something! He's—" she groped for words, "well, he's one of the most outstanding boys at school. He's terribly good-looking and all the girls are mad about him and he thinks I'm cute—at least that's what Ben says."

"But I've never seen him, have I?" Mom queried, the smile still contending with the frown on her face. "He's never been here? You've never had a date with him before?"

"Of course not," Midge sighed. "That's why it's so absolutely unbelievable that I'm going to the dance with him."

"But I haven't even heard you mention him," Mom persisted. "How do you suppose he happened to ask you to a big affair like the country-club dance?"

It was just a little deflating to have to admit, "Sandra had Ben fix up a double date for us. But it's all set and definite, they say. The whole crowd's going to the dance, you see, and then Sandra's having a supper party afterward at her house. And I'll need a new formal and——"

"Wait a minute," Mom interrupted. Her frown deepened and for just a moment Midge thought she might be taking exception to the idea of a new dress.

But then she said, "Honey, I don't like to spoil any part of this for you, but I'll want to know a little more about it all and I'm sure Dad will, too, before we say you can go."

"You mean—" Midge's tone was utterly aghast, "you might not let me?"

"I didn't say that," Mom corrected gently. "We'll just want to know more about it. You're not even sixteen yet, remember, and this sounds like a pretty grown-up sort of evening."

"What's that supposed to mean?" Midge demanded. "I've been to millions of dances before. What's so grown-up about a dance, for creep's sake?"

"You've been to school dances," Mom's tone was gently reasonable. "And you've gone with boys we know well—Bob, or Hans, not some complete stranger."

"Pete's all right!" Midge said flatly. "Just because he's terribly attractive and popular doesn't mean he isn't to be trusted. I never knew you to be so unreasonable! And a dance at the country club isn't anything shameful. There'll be all kinds of people there, old ones and young ones. Why in the world should you and Dad object to that?" She felt as though a rough hand were squeezing her heart, as if she were choking. The idea that her parents might take such an utterly unreasonable attitude about the whole thing simply had not occurred to her.

"Midge, listen," Mom said gravely. "I didn't say we'd object. I just want to know a little more about it all. You're the one who's being unreasonable, it seems to me. You know we've always trusted your judgment about friends, about things you want to do, just as we trusted Tobey and the older girls when they were your age. If you say this Pete is a nice boy, we'll take your word for it. And a dance at the country club may be all right too. But this party later at Sandra's," Mom's troubled glance was very direct on Midge's face, "that bothers me a little and I'm sure Dad will feel the same. Her parents seem so—casual about what she does, from all you've told me. Are you sure they'll be home the night she has this party?"

"Why," Midge stared back at her mother, "of course they'll be home! Or at least her mother will. I don't know about her father. But I'm sure they wouldn't let Sandra have a whole crowd of kids there with no grownups around at all. Why should you even think of such a thing?"

"Did Sandra say they'd be there?"

Never had Midge known Mom to be so unreasonably insistent. She answered, her tone level and a little withdrawn, "She didn't say, because I didn't ask. The subject didn't come up."

"Will you find out about it?" Mom queried.

"Yes, I will!" Midge said shortly. "And if her folks are going to be home, will it be all right if I go?"

Mom sighed. "I'll still have to talk it over with Dad," she told Midge. "I hate to seem such a spoilsport, but you really aren't as old as you imagine."

"Oh, honestly, Mother!" Midge said.

Turning on her heel, she went marching disgustedly up to her room.

147

CHAPTER 16

Party Plans

Midge asked Sandra the very next day whether her parents would be at home the night of her party.

"Why?" Sandra's dark brows rose mockingly. "Worried?"

"My mother is," Midge admitted a trifle uncomfortably.

"She's been reading too many articles about juvenile delinquents," Sandra said with a faint smile. "Is she afraid her sweet, innocent child may fall in with bad companions and there won't be any brave noble adults around to protect her?"

"Okay," Midge felt a prick of annoyance at Sandra's condescending attitude. "Just answer my question. Will they or won't they be home? If they won't," she added unhappily, "I can't come to the party at all."

"How do you stand being treated that way?" Sandra demanded. "As if you're a child, without any sense

148

or judgment of your own. I wouldn't put up with it, not for a minute!"

"My parents don't treat me like that," Midge told her. "They have lots of confidence in me. It's just—well, they don't want me to get involved in situations I haven't had enough experience to know how to cope with. I can see their viewpoint."

"I'm glad *you* can," Sandra scoffed. "It certainly isn't clear to me. How will you ever get any experience if they keep track of every little thing you do and won't trust you out of their sight without some other grownup around to watch you?"

"It's not like that at all." Loyalty to her parents, plus the warm love she felt for them, made Midge resent Sandra's attitude. Still, she didn't want to quarrel. She knew all the logical arguments in the world wouldn't alter Sandra's basic dislike and distrust of older people, so there was little point in trying to persuade her she was wrong. Past experience had taught Midge that. "Can't you just tell me whether your folks will be home that night," she coaxed, "without our getting into a great big hassle over it?"

Suddenly Sandra smiled with the winning sweetness which always melted Midge's defenses. "Of course they'll be home," she said. "They're going to the dance, too, and they may bring some friends back with them, but they'll be right here in the house with us. Do you suppose *that* will satisfy your parents, or shall I get a sworn statement in writing?"

"Very funny!" Midge said dryly. But she felt a lovely upsurge of relief just the same.

When, a few days later, she happened to encounter Pete Lovejoy in the corridor near her locker, she was elated to have him fall companionably into step with her after their initial greeting. "I hear we've got a date," he went on easily. "Is that okay with you?"

His grin was even more attractive and unnerving at close range than when seen at a distance. Still, Midge managed to gulp, her tone only slightly abnormal, "Oh, yes, if it is with you."

She was thankful she had worked on her parents so unremittingly that she had finally worn down their resistance. Of course the fact that Sandra's party was going to have adult supervision had helped a lot. With that much to build on, it hadn't been too hard to convince Mom and Dad that they should permit her to go to a country club dance with a crowd of her friends. After all, they wanted her to be happy. And they could see how vitally important this date was to her.

"Sure," Pete nodded, and Midge felt as though she were drowning in his bright, dark eyes, but she couldn't think of a more thrilling way to die. He asked then, "What color dress will you be wearing, so I'll know about flowers?"

"I'm not sure yet," Midge told him. "I'm going shopping for a new one today after school. Then I can let you know."

"No sweat," Pete said. "Plenty of time." He lifted a big hand in farewell as he left her at the door of the Math room.

Midge walked on air down the corridor toward her

next class, completely dazzled. She was scarcely touching ground several hours later when, as prearranged that morning, she met her mother in the misses' dress section of Wentworth's Department Store.

"This dress," she informed her mother solemnly, "must be absolutely perfect. It's for the most important date I've had in my whole, entire life."

Mom sighed. As the mother of four daughters, she had heard similar statements before. And they always preceded a long, difficult hunt. She and Midge looked and looked. Midge tried on and discarded one lovely dress after another. She was strongly drawn to an emerald-green cocktail dress, but her mother favored a pastel-blue net over taffeta.

"Mother!" Midge wailed. "I look about ten years old in it. Be reasonable!"

"The same to you," Mom said a trifle tartly. "In that green sheath you look like a little girl dressed up in something of her mother's!"

They compromised eventually on an embroidered organza in a subtle shade of blue-green which Midge considered only a little young and Mom only a little old. The full, ballerina-length skirt and artfully draped bodice were most becoming to Midge's tall slimness. And the more she looked at herself in the three-way mirror just outside the dressing room, the better she liked the effect. With long gloves and the right necklace, this might be even more effective than the green cocktail dress, she felt convinced.

"Midge, how lovely!" Tricia Farnham's enthralled

voice made her whirl in surprise. "I hope you're going to buy it."

"I've just about decided to," Midge nodded. "You really like it?" She was eager for the opinion of a contemporary.

"Oh, yes!" Tricia exclaimed. "I like it so well, it drew me from clear across the store. I was over in the next department, looking at sweaters, but I just had to have a closer look at this dress. And I didn't even know who had it on then."

Midge introduced Tricia to Mom and the three of them stood discussing the charms of the dress for a while longer. Then Midge went into the dressing room to change back into her own clothes. When she returned, her mother and Tricia were still talking. After the details of the purchase had been settled with the saleslady, Mom told Midge, "I want to do some Christmas shopping downstairs, but I'd rather you didn't come along. Do you mind?"

"Not if you buy me something elegant," Midge smiled.

"Why don't you come with me?" Tricia suggested to Midge. "I still want to find a sweater and maybe a blouse, if the sweater doesn't cost too much."

"Okay," Midge agreed. And Mom nodded and headed for the escalator.

While Midge helped Tricia look for a sweater, they chattered away without stopping. Talking with Tricia was almost as good as having Judy around again, Midge realized. Her growing liking for Tricia seemed to have dulled the earlier suspicions that had had their roots in Sandra's stories. It just didn't seem possible that Tricia was really the sort of person Sandra said she was. Of course, if Sandra were the one who was lying —Midge choked off the thought abruptly. What a thing to think about a friend!

Then another idea occurred to her. It was conceivable that Sandra might be mistaken about Tricia. Somehow Midge liked this notion much better. She could suspect that Sandra was mistaken without feeling disloyal toward her. It was even possible, Midge reflected, that if Sandra's trouble with Tricia had grown out of some sort of misunderstanding, then she might be able to straighten things out between them. She found this idea very appealing. But she would have to move carefully, with the greatest tact.

Toward this end, she tried to bring Sandra's name into their conversation. This wasn't hard to do, since, of course, Tricia was curious as to what special occasion Midge was buying a formal for. When Midge told her she meant to wear it at the Christmas dance, Tricia exclaimed, "Ooooh, lucky! I've never been to one of those. My parents don't belong to the country club and neither do Terry's. Are you going with Hans?"

"I'm going with Pete Lovejoy." Even as she said the words, Midge found them almost impossible to believe.

Tricia's brows rose and her lips formed a soundless whistle. "No wonder the occasion rates a new dress! If I didn't have Terry, I could envy you. Pete's really sharp."

"Yes, isn't he?" Midge's smile was dreamy. "Of course, I don't know him very well. This will be our first date. Sandra fixed it up for me. The whole crowd's going to the dance."

It seemed to Midge that Tricia's clear glance fell away from hers almost too quickly. She picked up a sweater from the counter before them and studied it carefully as she said, "I'm sure you'll have a wonderful time." Was Tricia's tone a little withdrawn, Midge wondered, or was she imagining that, too? Before she could decide, Tricia said with a faint sigh, "I don't believe there's a sweater here in the size and color I want. Shall we go see whether I can find a blouse?"

They had better luck in the blouse section. Tricia found a pink one she liked and bought it. Then, at Midge's suggestion, they stopped in the store's snack bar for a hot chocolate before going out into the chill gray day. Their conversation continued to run along easily, but Sandra's name didn't come up again. Each effort Midge made in that direction seemed to get nowhere. It soon became clear that Tricia was not going to say anything about Sandra, one way or another. It was as though, so far as she was concerned, the other girl simply didn't exist. This struck Midge as rather curious, since Sandra was so prone to talk about Tricia. But short of asking Tricia directly about her experience with Sandra, there seemed nothing further Midge could do. Better let the matter drop, she decided, before Tricia began to feel she was trying to pry into something which, actually, was none of her business.

Party Plans

The two girls lingered over their chocolate. Not since the day of the old-car rally had they spent so much uninterrupted time together, or had the opportunity for as long a conversation. And with each revelation of thought or feeling, the friendliness between them seemed to increase, the congeniality to deepen.

Later, breasting the cold wind together as they walked toward the corner where their homeward paths separated, Tricia remarked, "I'm having some kids over Friday night for a very informal party. Terry will be there, of course, and Jen and Bob and about half a dozen others. I'd love to have you and Hans come, too. Think you can make it?"

"I'd like to very much," Midge told her. "I imagine Hans would, too, if he's free."

"I'll call him when I get home," Tricia promised. "It won't be anything fancy, just ping-pong and dancing. Dad's rigged our hi-fi with a speaker in the basement."

"Sounds like fun," Midge smiled.

After they had said good-by and parted, Midge bent her head against the biting wind, edged now with tiny, sharp particles of snow, and hurried faster. Yet despite the weather, she felt pleasantly warm inside. And she hoped very hard that Hans would be free Friday night, that he'd like to go to a party.

Her mother had got home before her. Midge went out to the kitchen to help her get dinner started. As she peeled potatoes at the sink, she asked Mom, "How do you like Tricia?"

"She seems awfully nice," Mom answered. "So

friendly and full of fun. She reminds me quite a lot of her mother."

"I didn't know you knew Mrs. Farnham."

"We've been on committees together at Women's Club," Mom smiled. "I don't know her too well, but she's very pleasant."

Midge told Mom about the party Tricia had invited her and Hans to. "I hope he can make it. I'd like to go."

"It sounds like fun," Mom nodded.

"Tricia's going to call him, so I suppose she'll let me know——" Midge broke off at the sudden ring of the telephone. "Maybe that's she now!"

But it proved to be Hans, himself, calling to tell Midge he'd be delighted to take her to Tricia's party. Midge was just a little surprised at the rush of happiness that swept over her. For a girl who had a date for the Christmas dance with a wheel like Pete Lovejoy, she was getting a pretty large charge out of the prospect of spending an evening with Hans Dietrich. Sometimes lately it seemed to Midge she was finding herself a little hard to understand.

CHAPTER 17

Almost an Oddball

Tricia's party was even more fun than Midge had expected, yet just why she enjoyed it so thoroughly, she wasn't entirely sure. All they did was play ping-pong and talk and dance a little and eat hamburgers and chocolate cake. The Farnham basement was actually rather shabby, the masonry walls painted a light green, the furniture consisting of slightly sagging chairs and couches that had seen service abovestairs at some earlier time. Certainly it didn't compare with the Towerses' sumptuous rec room with its pine paneling, indirect lighting, and custom-built furniture.

Nor were the guests terribly outstanding. Most of them were kids Midge had known since her grade-school days. Yet the boys seemed much more intelligent and witty than she had realized they were, the girls were unaffectedly themselves. No one seemed to be trying to create an impression. All of them said what they thought and if their listeners didn't agree, they proceeded to say what they thought, and the argument grew heated and fascinating. Several times during the course of the evening the ping-pong players interrupted their game, the dancers turned off the record player, and everyone got involved in a serious discussion as to what was going on in the world and what should be done about it.

"It was so stimulating," Midge remarked to Hans as they walked home through a still world of snow and moonlight.

"I thought so too," Hans agreed. "I liked all those people very much. The talk reminded me of student discussions we often have at home in my country."

Midge frowned faintly. "The crowd I usually go around with never talk about anything serious. They think that's——" she broke off, groping for a word Hans would understand.

"Square?" he supplied, with a wry smile. "That is a word I have taken the trouble to learn, since I so often hear it."

"Yes, square," Midge smiled back. And suddenly she found herself pouring out to Hans some of the growing doubts and uncertainties she felt about Sandra's and the crowd's attitudes. "With them," she finished, "everything must be amusing, or else it's boring. Do you understand what I mean?"

"I think so," Hans nodded, his face grave in the moonlight. "But you are not like this. You must have little in common with them, really."

Midge spoke slowly, weighing each word, "It's as though there's a sort of pall over everything for them,

158

as though life itself is too dull to be borne, unless they work very hard at having fun every minute. Sandra doesn't believe in anything, actually, except the importance of *not* believing. She hasn't any sense of wonder or surprise. I really feel sorry for her."

"If you can help her, fine," Hans said. "But do not let her sickness infect you. From the things you say, I judge she is one of those people—and there are many in the world these days—who are afraid to feel, to reach out in warmth and kindness to their fellows. They set themselves apart from the rest of humanity, gathering about them a little group of people who distrust, who are equally bored with life. They think themselves above the norm, but they are to be pitied because they are turning their backs on their humanity in order to pursue something much less real, the illusion of their own greater importance."

Walking along beside Hans, talking and listening to his ideas, Midge felt herself closer to understanding Sandra and the rest of the crowd than she had ever been before. What troubled her was that with this greater understanding, her own acceptance of them and their ways seemed juvenile and unthinking.

But if this were so, Midge pursued the deflating thought still further, then it obviously followed that she had been very blind and stupid not to have seen before now that she really didn't fit in well with them. It would mean that Bob had been right, as had Tobey and her parents, and that she had been wrong. But she wasn't sure of that, Midge thought, retreating hastily from the conclusion toward which her thoughts

159

were pointing. She wasn't sure of it at all! This was probably just an idea engendered by being with a group of people so different from the crowd, of listening to Hans, as though he knew all about everything. Hans, too, could be wrong about Sandra and the others, she reminded herself firmly. After all, he scarcely knew them. Why should his opinion be so infallible?

Hans spoke, and again it was with that curious perception Midge had sensed in him before, as if he knew her thoughts even though she remained silent. He said, "Forgive me if I seem to talk about things which I should not, things that concern you and not me. I have no right to speak ill of your friends. I do not really mean to do so. If their ideas and attitudes are different from mine, this is not to say that they are wrong and I am correct. People are shaped by so many outside forces and influences—their parents, the sort of homes in which they grow up, their teachers and schools, the people they meet, their experiences. And our own personalities, our inner selves, may respond to these outside forces and influences in different ways, depending on the sort of persons we are. This is all a part of maturing, of developing into adult individuals capable of thinking for ourselves, of making up our own minds. Is it not so?"

Midge nodded. "Yes, I believe that too." Still an urge not to alienate herself from Sandra and the others, a need to belong to this group which was so exclusive and looked upon with envy by many, made her argue, "But there's really nothing wrong or bad about wanting to be popular and to have fun. We're at an age where these things are important. We needn't start taking life too seriously for a while yet."

"Of course not," Hans agreed. "We had fun tonight, though. A bit of serious conversation mixed in did not detract from that, would you say?"

Midge had to admit that it had not. In fact, the contrast had given the evening's lighter moments an increased aura of pleasure.

They had reached her door now and Hans said, smiling, "It has been a most pleasant evening. Thank you for sharing it with me, Midge."

"I enjoyed it too," Midge told him.

Her heart beat faster as he put an arm around her shoulders and laid his cold cheek for a moment against hers. There was a rather unsettling tenderness in the gesture. But he didn't follow it up by kissing her, although Midge thought for a moment that he meant to. But he merely said good night and strode off down the street, as Midge let herself into the house. The warm melting softness inside her made her suspect strongly that she would have let him kiss her had he tried to. Maybe it would happen next time.

Midge slept late that Saturday morning and wandered downstairs in her robe and slippers around ten o'clock. Mom was running the vacuum cleaner in the living room, but she turned it off at the sound of Midge's cheery, "Good morning."

"So you finally made it," Mom smiled. "Did you have fun last night?"

161

"Um-hum! Has everybody eaten? I thought I smelled pancakes."

"You did," Mom nodded, "and there's plenty of batter left. Pork sausages too. Dad and I ate earlier. He had to go downtown to the bank."

"Come have a cup of coffee with me," Midge invited, "and I'll fill you in on all the details about last night."

She proceeded to do so while she ate a hearty breakfast and Mom lingered companionably over her coffee across the table. It was fun sharing experiences with Mom, she was always so interested and enthusiastic.

When Midge finished her recital, Mom said, "It sounds as though you had a fine time." She added then, with a faint smile, "It also sounds as though you're beginning to like Hans pretty well."

"You mean it shows that plainly?"

As they laughed together, Mom told her, "I don't blame you a bit. Dad and I think he's quite an exceptional young man."

"He fitted into that bunch last night awfully well," Midge said thoughtfully. "They're all rather unusual. I mean they aren't afraid of seeming square or corny. They stand up for what they think, even when the argument gets hot and heavy. It's sort of exciting. I haven't been around that sort of kids often before. But I liked them a lot. Even old Bob. He has some very intelligent ideas."

"I've always known Bob was intelligent," Mom said.

"Tricia just seemed to spark the whole thing," Midge went on. "The better I get to know her, the more I like her. I can't help thinking," she confided, "that Sandra's mistaken about her. Oh, I don't mean she's deliberately saying anything untrue—but she could be wrong."

"Of course she could," Mom agreed. "It's best to find out about people for yourself, not accept someone else's opinion."

"I don't see why I can't be friends with both of them," Midge said slowly. "I like them both."

"Then I should think you could," Mom nodded. "The more friends, the better, I'd figure."

But Sandra, Midge was to find out very shortly, had other ideas. She was avid for details of Tricia's party and, when Midge supplied them, she laughed a small, supercilious laugh and said, "Maybe that'll teach you not to waste your time on a bunch of oddballs."

"But I had fun," Midge insisted. "Maybe I'm a little on the oddball side too. I certainly felt right at home." She didn't add, "More at home than I often feel with our crowd." But the words formed in her mind and she frowned at the realization.

"Even if you are a little that way," Sandra said sharply, "you can get over it. You have to make an effort, though."

"Why?"

"Because oddballs," Sandra informed her, "do not fit into our crowd. The important kids at school don't go for them. You know that as well as I do. You're just being perverse about it."

"I feel perverse," Midge admitted. Maybe being with Hans and Tricia and the others had made rebel-

163

lion grow in her. She was a little surprised now at the strength of it. "None of our crowd," she went on, "thinks too highly of me, I'm afraid. They just put up with me because of you. I've never been invited to any of the other girls' parties. The boys take me out once, when you have Ben fix up a double date, and then that's the end of it. All they really do is tolerate me."

"It's because you don't try to fit in," Sandra accused. "You don't make enough effort. The Christmas dance will change things, you'll see. The fact that you're going to it and to my party with a wheel like Pete Lovejoy—none of the crowd can ignore that. You'll be all set after next Saturday."

Next Saturday! Midge had almost forgotten how close was this important date in her life. Her first big dance at the country club, her first date with Pete, her first chance to go to one of the crowd's parties— how could she have let a simple little get-together at Tricia's house overshadow all that? And why, she asked herself further, should she risk Sandra's friendship and approval by being so belligerent and unreasonable at a time like this? It simply didn't make sense!

"I hope so," Midge heard her own voice agreeing meekly with Sandra's last statement.

But deep within her a strange sense of ferment, of confusion, made her wonder whether she truly wanted to be "all set" with Sandra's crowd. Or would she rather be accepted by the crowd she had been with the other night at Tricia's party?

The deciding factor in the matter seemed to be Pete Lovejoy. The thought of him was all it took to make Midge's uncertainty fade.

The dreadful to be in the matter seemed to be
Why I am we. The thought of him was all it too
to even Midge's mounting fade...

CHAPTER 18

The Christmas Dance

The Christmas dance, scheduled as it was for the Saturday before Christmas, would fall on the day that also began the two-week holiday from school. For this Midge was grateful, since that last week of classes seemed unusually hectic. Maybe the teachers didn't actually vie with each other in loading on homework, still, between doing her own and the greater share of Sandra's, Midge felt swamped. Besides, she had Christmas shopping to take care of, gifts to wrap and hide away in the Heydons' already bulging closets. Midge had always loved this preholiday time, with its rush and excitement, its growing suspense, the warm atmosphere of good will that prevailed. She still loved it, but this year something seemed to be lacking. And she had a troubling suspicion that this lack was in herself.

Was this dullness, this queer unrest, this feeling of being pulled two ways a part of growing up, she won-

166

dered? Or did it stem from her inability to make up her mind about Sandra and Tricia? Sometimes she felt strongly drawn to Tricia; she wanted to be one of the oddballs, as Sandra derisively called them, who were Tricia's and Terry's friends. Then again, when envious admiration lighted the eyes of classmates as she and Sandra walked together along the hall at school, Midge would think she was out of her mind remotely to consider giving up such prestige. Even if she didn't always agree with Sandra, even if she sometimes found the crowd snobbish and superficial, Midge felt she was lucky to be accepted by them. This was especially true with the dance and her date with Pete Lovejoy looming excitingly ahead.

As the big day drew near, Midge found it easier to concentrate on it and shut other troubling matters out of her thoughts. Rather disappointingly, her contact with Pete at school remained completely casual. Midge had told him the color of her dress and he had asked whether a white corsage might not be best with it. Midge agreed that it would. But other than that one conversation, all they did was say hello when they happened to meet in the corridor.

"You'd hardly know we were going to have a date," Midge complained wistfully to Sandra. "I hope he doesn't forget it."

"Football players are usually inarticulate," Sandra comforted. "But he's a sharp dancer."

"I know," Midge nodded. "I've seen him." The thought of actually dancing with Pete left her breathless.

At last the interminable week ended, school was over for two glorious holiday weeks, and the day of the dance was thrillingly at hand. No wonder Midge felt totally disassociated from reality, caught up in a fairy tale.

It took her practically all day Saturday to get ready for the dance. In the morning she washed and set her hair, then gave herself a manicure and a pedicure as well. She experimented with eye shadow, although her mother took a dim view of this.

"You won't even look like yourself," she told Midge. "If you use any, it's going to be only the tiniest touch." And she added, "Honestly, when I was your age, my mother barely permitted me to use face powder."

"That was in the olden days," Midge teased. A sudden irresistible impulse made her go to her mother, put her arms about her and bury her face against the comfortable softness of her shoulder. Something almost like fear washed over her. But there was nothing to be afraid of, for creep's sake. She was only going to a dance with a new boy. She brushed her mother's cheek with a slightly embarrassed kiss and said, "That's for being so understanding about everything!"

"If I weren't fairly understanding after having had four daughters to enlighten me," Mom smiled, patting Midge's arm, "I'd be a little stupid, wouldn't I?" Then her smile faded and a faint frown wrinkled her brow. "Midge, you're not worried about tonight, are you?"

"Why should I be worried?" Midge made her tone casual, but it took a bit of effort.

168

"I don't know," Mom said. "I just get the impression you're rather tense. I wish you were going with Hans."

"That's because you haven't seen Pete," Midge told her. "Half the girls at school would give anything to be in my shoes tonight."

"He isn't one of those wild, show-off drivers, is he?"

"I don't know," Midge admitted, "but we're going in Ben's car. You know he drives okay."

"I'm glad of that," Mom sighed.

Midge was much too excited to do more than pick at her dinner. "I never thought I'd see the day when anything affected your appetite," her father grinned across the table at her.

"Don't worry." Midge's answering smile was a little unsteady. "There'll be refreshments at the dance and still more to eat at Sandra's later. I won't starve." She thought to remind Dad then, "When Pete picks me up, please don't tell him I've got to be home by one o'clock. I'll let him know later. And please——"

"Don't tell him to drive carefully," her father took the words out of her mouth. "I won't, honey. I understand he isn't going to do the driving, or I might be tempted. But I promise to be on my very best behavior. Okay?"

"Okay," Midge nodded. "I wasn't really worried."

Pete was calling for her at nine, which left her plenty of time to bathe and dress and fuss over her face and hair, to apply her most seductive perfume in all the logical places. Mom came in to help adjust her dress over the bouffant crinoline petticoat and to check on her stocking seams. And Dad stuck his head around the edge of the door for a preview.

"You look beautiful," he told her, his voice a little gruff, "but isn't it rather low?"

"Dad, it's very conservative," Midge whirled from the mirror to face him, her eyes sparkling. "You should see Sandra's."

"I probably couldn't stand the shock," Dad said dryly. "And how are you ever going to walk in those heels?" He turned toward Mom accusingly, "What were you thinking of, to let her buy shoes like that?"

"It's the only type of heels you can find on evening slippers," Mom defended herself. "And she says all the girls wear them."

"Kids grow up too soon nowadays," Dad wagged his head disapprovingly. "Why, when we were fifteen——"

"I'm practically sixteen," Midge reminded him softly.

"Even that is not a ripe old age." Dad frowned. "Just remember what I told you about getting home by one. And see that this fellow you're going with understands I mean it."

"I will," Midge promised. "Don't worry."

Mom said gently, "She'll be all right, Henry. She's really quite sensible. And she says Pete is——" she broke off as the doorbell sounded.

Midge cried, in a choked tone, "He's here now! Please go on down and let him in. And be nice to him. I'll come in just a minute."

She clenched her hands so hard her nails actually

hurt her palms, as her parents hurried downstairs. Her heart pounded heavily. There was the sound of the door opening, then a polite murmur of voices reached her ears, diminishing as her parents took Pete into the living room. Midge closed her eyes for a minute, then opened them for a last, reassuring look at herself in the mirror. Nothing appeared lacking, at least not to the naked eye. If only Pete thought so too, Midge hoped.

She went downstairs carefully in her unaccustomedly high heels. What an entrance it would be if she tripped and fell flat on her face! The thought made her smile and she was still smiling as she reached the door of the living room and looked in at the rather stiff tableau presented by her parents, sitting side by side on the couch, while Pete Lovejoy, looking absolutely wonderful in dinner jacket and black bow tie, seemed perched for flight on the extreme edge of a chair, a little plastic box clutched in his hands.

Her father must have asked him something about football, because as Midge came in Peter was saying, "—best halfback will graduate this June, so I don't know how next year's team——" he broke off at the sound of Midge's approach and got politely to his feet to greet her. "Boy!" he exclaimed, and it did Midge's heart good to see the appreciation that lighted his dark eyes. "Here," he handed her the corsage box, "add this to the effect."

"Thanks," Midge's voice was husky. She stared down at the first orchid anyone had ever given her—and a white one, at that! "It's just beautiful, Pete. I'm going to carry it this way, though, till we get there, so it won't be crushed."

"Okay," he nodded. "Let's put the show on the road."

"I'll get my coat," Midge told him as they moved toward the hall, her parents trailing along.

Mom and Dad said the usual things. "Have a wonderful time." And, "Isn't it nice the weather stayed clear?" Pete's answers were courteous. He helped Midge into her coat, then shrugged on his own. With a final flurry of good-bys, Midge and he went out into the chill, starlit night and shut the door behind them. It was almost, Midge thought rapturously, like a curtain going up on a long anticipated play. Only she wasn't a mere spectator, she was right in the midst of it! She drew a deep, deep breath and the cold made her chest hurt a little, as Pete took her arm chummily.

"Grrr," he emitted a mock-ferocious growl. "You smell good. What is it, Canal Number Five, or Ditchwater Ten?"

Midge laughed appreciatively, then felt her fingers almost crushed in Pete's hard grip, as he released her elbow at the foot of the steps and caught her hand instead.

Suddenly her eyes widened. The car parked on the drive wasn't Ben's red convertible, but a light-gray sedan, completely strange to her and quite empty. "I thought Ben was taking us," she said doubtfully. "Sandra said so."

"Don't believe everything you hear," Pete chuckled,

helping her in and going around to the other side of the car to slide under the wheel. "You girls would have been too crowded in those full dresses. Besides, it'll be better to have two cars for later. Why, do you mind?"

Midge shook her head, her smile a little forced. She didn't mind, really. It was just that she had told her parents—but they'd understand when she explained how it was. They'd know she hadn't meant to lie about it. She said, "It doesn't really matter. I was just surprised, that's all."

"I'm a surprising guy," Pete said, his voice low and thrillingly intimate. "You're sort of surprising too. You've got assets in that dress that I never suspected. But we'll have a good chance to get acquainted tonight. *Real* well acquainted."

"I—guess we will," Midge murmured.

She chattered away, trying to be vivaciously amusing, as Pete drove conservatively through residential streets until they reached the highway. Once there, he pushed the car to a rate of speed Midge found appalling, although Pete was so relaxed and at ease behind the wheel it seemed foolish to worry.

"Aren't we going pretty fast?" Midge queried.

"What are you, a back-seat driver or something?" Pete's tone was airy. "I'm watching the mirror for any signs of the law. I got a speeding ticket last month, which made the old man pretty sore. He warned me if I ever played chicken again, he wouldn't let me take the car out of the garage. Sounded as if he meant it, too, so I've been behaving. This is nothing."

Midge felt relieved when they reached the country club parking lot and found a spot near Ben's red convertible. "You'll get your shoes dirty in this gravel," Pete warned. "Wait a sec."

He went around and opened the car door for Midge, then swung her up into his arms as easily as though she were a child. He carried her to the edge of the paved drive that led to the club entrance. "There you are," he grinned down at her.

"Thanks," Midge answered, her heart beating fast, her smile a little tremulous. A wonderful, warm glow enveloped her. It had been thrilling, feeling Pete's arms close about her, his cheek near hers. Lots of boys his age drove too fast and were inclined to be reckless. It scarcely seemed fair to hold it against him. She put the thought of it out of her mind as they climbed the broad stone steps and entered the brightly lighted clubhouse.

Lively music, animated voices, and laughter reached their ears. And Midge's eyes widened in appreciation of the color and movement all about. Checking their wraps took only a moment, and Pete obligingly held up her compact mirror so she could see to pin on the lovely orchid corsage. Then arm in arm they made their way into the big, brilliantly decorated ballroom, where a dance was just ending. Sandra's voice hailed them and, as Midge and Pete moved to join the other members of the crowd congregating in a gay clump in the corner, Midge had never known a sharper sense of pleasure, of anticipation.

It was going to be a wonderful night!

174

CHAPTER 19

A Hard Lesson

Pete was indeed a wonderful dancer. The only trouble was, he held Midge considerably closer than she was accustomed to being held and, while this was undeniably exciting, it tended to make her stiffen just a little.

"Come on, baby, relax," Pete coaxed, his lips close to her ear. "I won't bite. What are you afraid of?"

"N-nothing," Midge said, sharply annoyed with the slight tremor in her voice.

"Warm up then," Pete said, "and let's enjoy ourselves."

Maybe she was being unreasonable, Midge thought. Sandra and Ben danced past, locked in an embrace quite as close as that in which she was held. And Sandra obviously didn't mind. Her eyes were half shut and a slight smile curved her mouth.

Pete must have noticed them, too, because he said,

"See, they're feeling no pain at all. That's how you do it."

Midge tried to dance more easily, but Pete's arm was like a vise about her. She couldn't help pulling a little away from him. And she was secretly relieved when the long dance was over and the orchestra signaled a break.

Pete's hand under her elbow guided her toward a deep couch in a corner where their crowd was congregating. Debbie Burke, striking in bright red, was with Norm Hagen, Sharon Cutler, her pale blond hair piled high, clung ardently to Hoyt Paxton's arm. There were several other couples, all of whom greeted Midge and Pete in friendly fashion. A warm sense of pleasure, of belonging, rose in Midge. Here with the others, the queer feeling of strain that had troubled her lessened.

"That was a pretty hot number," Ben said, mopping his forehead. "Anyone else need a drink?"

"Now you're talking," Pete said with enthusiasm.

Several of the other boys also accepted Ben's offer. They murmured excuses and headed for the nearest exit.

"Ben came prepared," Sandra smiled knowingly. "He knew they wouldn't serve them at the bar."

"Doesn't he always come prepared?" Sharon drawled. "You'd think his father would realize his supply is dwindling."

"He's usually too stoned to notice," Sandra said. She added then, "and speaking of *that*, there go my parents, heading for the bar."

176

Midge followed the direction of Sandra's glance and saw Sandra's mother, accompanied by a handsome, heavy-set man, disappearing through a doorway on the far side of the room.

"That's the first time I've ever seen your father," she told Sandra.

"Is it?" Sandra asked. "You probably won't see him any more tonight either. At least, not dancing. He doesn't come to dances to dance," she added lightly, "although my mother enjoys it. But Dad's natural habitat is the bar."

Everyone laughed at this but Midge. She couldn't help wondering whether Sandra really considered it as funny as she tried to make it sound.

As soon as the music started again, the boys came back. There was an unmistakable hint of liquor on Pete's breath, Midge noticed, but he didn't hold her quite so close this dance, so she actually enjoyed it more.

"Old Ben's been giving me advice," Pete confided. "He said never rush a girl and you'll get farther. Me, I'm a man of action, but I have to admit Ben knows how to handle women. So I'm trying it his way."

"Why do you say he knows how to handle women?" Midge asked.

"Because he's got Sandra eating out of his hand," Pete explained. "That's quite an accomplishment, believe me!"

Midge wondered whether his impressed tone indicated he envied Ben. But if that were so, she'd rather not be sure of it.

177

During the next intermission a big discussion arose as to whether the crowd should leave after one more number and go to Sandra's house.

"But we just got here," Midge objected.

"The music's so awful, though," Debbie complained.

It had seemed fine to Midge.

"And the place is so full of old people," Sandra said. "There aren't many kids our age here. Let's not stay much longer."

"I'd like to have a couple more dances," Sharon put in.

And Pax, his arm around her, seconded, "Sure, let's stick around a little while. Your old man won't feel he got his money's worth, paying for all the guest tickets, if we leave too soon. He'll think we're ungrateful."

"He'd never know the difference," Sandra drawled, "once he gets in that bar."

Midge stared at her, a faint frown wrinkling her forehead. "But they're going home when we do, aren't they?" she asked. "You told me——"

"Yes, of course," Sandra assured her. "I'll let my mother know when we're ready to leave."

"How come?" Ben asked.

Sandra's glance met his for a moment. Then she said reprovingly, "Why, Ben, you know they wouldn't let me have a party without their being at home."

"Of course not!" Debbie exclaimed.

Sandra went on hurriedly, "We'll stay for two more dances and then leave. Okay with you all?"

The music started up once more, drowning out the

178

murmur of agreement. This time it was a fast number with a decided beat, and the floor was almost entirely taken over by the younger dancers, whirling and twisting, separating to arm's length, coming together again, their faces as gravely intent as though they were performing some mystic rite. Midge thoroughly enjoyed it. Pete's hand was so firm on hers, his steps so intricate, yet not hard to follow. In the heady pleasure of the dance she forgot about the faint uneasiness that had stirred in her as the others talked during the intermission. Now her only regret was that they were going to leave so soon. But of course it would be fun to go on to Sandra's party.

The Towerses' house was less than a mile from the club. Still, Midge felt relieved when it developed that Debbie and Norm wanted to ride back there with Pete and her. "I got all crushed in that little car of Pax's as we came," Debbie complained, "and you've got a whole empty back seat!" She and Norm settled down in it cozily.

"Stowaways!" Pete accused. "Oh, well, if you must, you must, I suppose. But don't count on riding home with us later. We'll want privacy, won't we, baby?" His arm went around Midge, pulling her close against him on the wide front seat.

A slight shiver ran through her. She couldn't think of anything to say.

Norm answered, his voice slightly muffled, "We'll worry about that when the time comes." And that was the last word from the back seat all the way to Sandra's house.

179

Midge tried to keep up a conversation as they drove along. She would have preferred that Pete use both hands to drive with, but when she rather hesitantly suggested it, he only laughed. "Don't worry. I'm an expert. What's the matter? Don't you like me?"

"Of course," Midge gulped.

It would be better, she told herself, when they reached Sandra's. Then the whole crowd would be together again, and somehow Pete seemed more attractive to her in a crowd. Sandra had told her parents they were leaving the club. Midge had seen her talking with her mother in the doorway of the bar. And Sandra had returned to say that her parents would gather some friends together and take them back to their house for drinks.

But the older people hadn't got there yet when Sandra and the others congregated in the brightly lighted rec room. There was no sign of anyone at all about the place. Agnes, having arranged a variety of fancy food on a long buffet table, had apparently gone to bed. But Sandra's parents and their friends were bound to be along soon, Midge assured herself.

No one else seemed in the least bothered by anything. In fact their spirits were even higher now than they had been at the club. Someone put a stack of records on the hi-fi and dance music poured out into the room. Some of the couples gathered around the table, helping themselves to sandwiches and relishes and potato chips. There was a big cooler filled with ice and soft drinks.

When Midge reached for a bottle of ginger ale to

go with her sandwich, Pete said in an appalled tone, "You're not going to drink that stuff straight, I hope! It's poison that way. Hey, Sandra, where does your old man keep his liquor?"

"Right over there under the bar," Sandra informed him.

"Well, make like a hostess and get us some," Ben told her. "He might not like it if we just helped ourselves."

Sandra laughed and crossed the room to the pine-paneled bar. "Here you are," she said, returning with two bottles which she set down with a thump on the long table. Her eyes caught Midge's then, and at the look in them Sandra frowned mockingly and said to Ben, "Take it easy. You're shocking Midge. And we don't want to do anything like that, now, do we?"

"Depends on how easily she shocks," Norm Hagen said, pouring liquor into the bottom of his glass and filling it up with ginger ale.

"I don't want any," Midge said, when Pete started to fill a glass for her. "I mean, I just want plain ginger ale."

"A teetotaler!" Pete exclaimed, chuckling. "We'll have to cure you of that!"

Not all of the crowd added liquor to their drinks, Midge noted. But the ones who didn't seemed entirely unconcerned over the ones who did. Was it adult to be tolerant in such a situation, she wondered, to accept it casually and not let it spoil your fun? She felt uncertain and confused, never having been faced with such a situation before. She was troubled, too, by the fact that there had been no slightest sound of Sandra's parents and their friends arriving. How long were they going to take, she wondered? If they didn't come fairly soon, she would ask Sandra about it, she decided. After all, she didn't want to be put into the position of having lied to Mom and Dad.

"You know what the trouble is around here?" Debbie, dancing with her cheek close against Norm's, queried. "It's much too light."

"Now you're talking," several voices agreed from all sides of the room. And Ben suggested, "Shall I douse 'em, Sandy?"

"By all means," Sandra laughed. "Agnes always turns on every one in the place. I don't think she trusts us!"

There was a burst of laughter at this and Ben started a systematic tour, turning off lamps and pressing light switches as he went, until the big room was in complete darkness except for a shaft of light that shone faintly from the stairs.

"That's much better," Pete said, coming up behind Midge and putting his arms around her. "Now we can get somewhere."

Midge felt as though she were stifling and her heart began to thump heavily. Pete's arms gathered her closer, turning her toward him. All about, as her eyes grew accustomed to the sudden dimness, she was aware of couples settling cozily in the deep chairs and couches, or just standing locked in a close embrace.

She tried to strain away from Pete, but he was too strong. His face came inexorably closer and Midge was aware of the smell of the liquor he had drunk,

182

mingled with the shaving lotion she had thought so pleasant earlier in the evening. Now she felt sick and shaken and filled with such a frantic urge to escape his grip, the threatened touch of his lips on hers, that she would have done anything at all to break free. "Let me go!" she exclaimed.

But Pete only laughed. "What a wildcat!"

Suddenly Midge didn't care what he thought of her; she didn't care if she never saw him again. She didn't care if she never saw Sandra, either, or any of the rest of the crowd. In this moment of startling clarity, she realized at last how blindly foolish she had been to be impressed with them for even a little while.

"If you don't let me go," she told Pete through clenched teeth, "you'll be sorry." Then, as he continued to hold her, she drew back one foot and gave him a sharp kick on the shin with her pointed-toed slipper. The impact hurt her foot, so she wasn't surprised to hear Pete emit a yelp of pain and to feel his grip loosen.

"You little devil!" he accused. "What's the idea?"

Now everyone was staring at them. Midge could feel eyes boring into her from the dimness all around the room. But she didn't care. She was going to say what she thought at last and she was going to say it right out loud for everyone to hear.

She told Sandra, "If this is the kind of parties you go in for, I'm not coming to any more of them!"

"Now aren't you ashamed," Sandra drawled mockingly to Pete. "You've frightened the poor baby."

"Frightened her!" Pete growled. "She practically broke my leg. Did you see that kick she gave me?"

"I'm not frightened," Midge insisted hotly, "I'm disgusted. With you," she told Pete, her eyes flashing, "and all the rest of you." Her accusing glance sought Sandra. "You don't even care whether your parents come home, do you? After telling me so positively they'd be here."

Sandra shrugged. "If they prefer to go somewhere else, or stay on at the club, why should I care? I don't need them."

Midge stared at her, not liking what she saw so clearly now, both in Sandra and the others. They had seemed to stand for so much to her, but, in reality, they stood for very little. She realized that at last. Without another word she turned and started toward the stairs.

"If you're going home," Pete sneered, "I suppose I'll have to take you. It's too far to walk."

"I'm going to call my father," Midge informed him. "He'll come and get me. I wouldn't go with you for anything!"

There was a shout of laughter behind her at this. Midge felt her cheeks flame. But it wasn't because she minded being laughed at by the crowd. Her embarrassment was for her own stupidity in not seeing through Sandra and the others long before this. Now that she realized the sort they were, it shamed her to remember how dazzled she had been by them.

But by the time she reached the telephone and started dialing the familiar number, she had decided she ought to be grateful to them for teaching her a lesson.

184

CHAPTER 20

Christmas Ahead

Her phone call completed, Midge found her coat and started toward the door. She didn't want to stay in this house a moment longer. But Sandra's voice stopped her.

"So you're actually going." She had apparently followed Midge upstairs, moved by some desire for a final, private word. Now as Midge turned in surprise to face her, the other girl's tone grew taunting. "You're being an awful baby, you know."

"I don't think so," Midge denied.

"Pete will never forgive you," Sandra warned.

"I don't care," Midge said flatly. "I don't care what any of you think of me. Not now. Not ever."

"How can you be so silly?" Sandra asked pityingly. "Aren't you even a little bit grown-up?"

Their eyes met and held and Midge realized that she was seeing Sandra with complete clarity for the first time. The ache of disillusionment was sharp in her throat as she answered, "There are different definitions of the word." Then, turning, she let herself out into the starry darkness, closing the door firmly behind her.

The cold air felt clean and fresh and oddly comforting as she walked down the long drive and waited at the end of it for her father. He came in a very short time, hair tousled, overcoat and trousers pulled on hastily over his pajamas. Not until Midge was sitting beside him, his arm comfortingly around her shoulders, did the tears she had been holding back begin to squeeze from underneath her eyelids.

"There, honey," Dad said gently, although his face was unaccustomedly stern in the dimness of the car. "It's all right."

"I know," Midge brushed the tears away with the back of her hand. There was nothing to cry about now. It must be some sort of emotional reaction to the scene she had been through.

"I ought to go in there," Dad eyed the beautiful house wrathfully, "and tell that young punk what I think of him!"

Midge's lips twisted in a shaky smile. "There's no need of that. I told them all what I thought of them —that's enough."

"But Sandra's parents," Dad frowned, "how can they be so irresponsible? A crowd of kids there and no grownups around at all—they're just asking for trouble."

"I know," Midge agreed, "but we can't do anything about it. Maybe they'll be along soon. I—just hate

186

being put into the spot of having lied to you and Mom. I didn't mean to."

"We know that," Dad assured her, giving her shoulder a final pat and driving the car away from the curb. "We're not blaming you at all. We're only glad you called us."

"Did I wake up Mom too?" Midge's voice was steadier.

Dad nodded. "She'd have come with me, only she didn't want to take the time to dress. She'll be waiting for us, though."

During the short drive, and later on at home with both her parents, Midge explained how the evening had grown increasingly disappointing, reaching its climax in Pete's objectionable attitude.

"He always seemed nice at school," Midge said ruefully. "I had no idea he was such a wolf."

But she didn't dwell merely on Pete. What she wanted to make clear to her parents was the insight she had gained, not only into Sandra's character, but into her own as well. "You were right," she told them, "and so were Tobey and Bob—all the people who tried to make me see that Sandra and I could never be real friends. I'm through with that whole crowd now. I told them so tonight. I guess I just had to learn," she finished, "that the right crowd to belong to is the one in which you, personally, fit best, not just the smoothest one that outsiders envy and admire."

"I'm proud of you," Dad said quietly. "It takes courage to admit you've been mistaken."

And Mom added, "It takes courage, too, to stand

up and say what you think to a lot of people who have other ideas."

Feeling their love and warm approval wrapping her about, Midge didn't even mind admitting, "I suppose, though, Sandra will think of some story to explain it all to her advantage. I'm quite sure now that's what she must have done when Tricia Farnham got fed up with her. But I don't really care what she says about me. Somehow it doesn't seem important any more."

"People who know you won't believe her if what she says isn't true," Mom pointed out.

"I'm not worried," Midge smiled.

Rather surprisingly, she found she really meant it. Tricia and Terry would understand the situation and so would Hans and Bob. When you got right down to it, there were a great many more kids at school who would be unswayed by Sandra's opinions than would accept them as true. Looked at from a broad perspective, Sandra probably wasn't nearly as important as she thought she was.

Suddenly a thought struck Midge and she laughed quietly. "I wonder whom she'll get to do her homework next?" she said. "Now that I've seen the light, she'll have to find someone, or else do it herself. And she wouldn't like that a bit."

A sort of buoyancy swelled in Midge, making her feel almost lightheaded. A weight seemed to have slipped from her shoulders. All the doubts and uncertainties that had warred in her these past weeks were quiet now. The knowledge that she was through with Sandra and with all the crowd that followed her lead so slavishly brought in its wake a sharp, sweet sense of relief.

Midge called Tricia on Sunday afternoon and asked her to come over. The other girl accepted with pleasure, and half an hour later the two sat talking confidentially in Midge's room. Midge told Tricia frankly of her disillusionment with Pete and of her final break with Sandra. She didn't go into great detail; still, she felt sure Tricia grasped the situation. "I guess I should have seen before this that I didn't belong in that crowd," Midge admitted.

"It took me quite a while, too," Tricia said with a rueful smile. "They're pretty dazzling till you see through them."

Neither girl spoke unkindly of Sandra, although she had taken advantage of them in much the same way. Actually they rather pitied her. Maybe she couldn't help being the sort of person she was, with the background she had, the lack of close family ties and understanding. Still, the awareness of their similar treatment at her hands only served to strengthen the genuine liking that existed between them and which had already begun to develop into a warm and lasting friendship.

Midge found herself looking forward to the rest of the holidays with happy anticipation. On Christmas Eve Tobey and Brose would get home and the traditional family celebration would begin. Almost every day Midge saw Tricia, or talked with her on the phone. And now that the inner conflict which had torn her had been resolved, Midge's old zest and enjoyment of the season surged up strongly once more.

Early that week she had an amusing Christmas card from Tom Brooks, with a letter enclosed in it. He seemed very real in her mind as she read it through. Next summer if they got together, as Tom seemed so confident they would, she must tell him of her experiences trying to fit into a smooth crowd. She could almost hear Tom hooting with laughter. But she was very sure he would approve of what she'd done.

On the morning of the day before Christmas Midge answered the phone and was delighted to hear Hans's voice. "Are you too busy with holiday preparations to do something for a couple of hours?" he asked hopefully.

"I've got all my gifts wrapped," Midge told him, "and Mom and I finished the cookies yesterday. Why, what did you have in mind?"

"Have you ever gone skiing?" His voice was boyishly enthusiastic.

"No, I haven't," Midge had to admit.

"Would you like to?" Hans queried. "I can borrow some skis for you and I brought mine from Germany with me. I should like very much to teach you to ski this morning."

"Well, fine," Midge agreed. "But where will we go?"

"The small hill back of the high school," Hans informed her, "will be quite high enough for a beginner like you."

At Hans's suggestion Midge dressed in slacks and

190

windbreaker, warm mittens and earmuffs. The two of them trudged off happily toward the school, the long, polished pairs of skis slung across Hans's shoulder. In his bright, heavy knitted sweater and beaked cap he looked attractive and assured.

"Who knit that gorgeous sweater for you?" Midge asked. "The girl you left behind?"

"I suppose you could say that," Hans nodded gravely, but with a gleam of humor in his glance. "My mother."

Midge hoped the relief she felt at his words didn't show.

The next hours were great fun. Midge fell again and again, but the snow was powdery and soft and Hans's grip was firm, helping her to her feet. He was so skillful and graceful, negotiating the gentle slope himself, Midge would have been content just to watch him. But he was determined she should learn how to do it, and he proved an able and patient instructor.

"Now you are getting it," he told her jubilantly, when she managed to glide down the little hill three times in a row without mishap. "I'll make a skier of you yet. But we should stop now. I don't want you feeling stiff and sore tomorrow."

As they headed for home, Midge told him, "Hans, I've made up my mind about some things that were bothering me."

"That is good," he smiled down at her.

"Tricia and I," Midge went on, "have become closer friends than ever. And I've decided I really fit in best with that crowd of hers, the kids we had so much fun with the night of her party."

"And what of your smooth friends?" Hans queried. "How do Sandra and the others feel about this?"

"They've dropped me," Midge laughed. "But I had the fun of dropping them first, so I don't care."

Hans clapped an approving hand on her shoulder and Midge felt her heart beat in a faster rhythm at his touch. "I am glad," he said, "that you have found out for yourself where you belong, where you will be happiest. This is important." He added then, his tone a shade deeper and his blue eyes grave on her face, "I hope I, too, may fit into this new circle you've decided to be a part of."

"Oh, you do," Midge assured him. "You fit in very well."

As his eyes held hers for a long, revealing moment, she tried to decide quickly whether she liked him better than Tom, or Tom better than he. But she liked them both so well, it was extremely hard to make up her mind. Really, Midge thought, a smile curving her mouth, at this stage it wasn't so important to be absolutely sure. There was lots of time. Just knowing two boys like Hans and Tom was wonderful. And, when you got right down to it, life was pretty wonderful, too.

1540